Back to Bayfield

A No Place Like Home Romance

Back to Bayfield

Back to Bayfield

A No Place Like Home Romance

Elaine Koyama

Back to Bayfield

Copyright © 2024 by Elaine Koyama

All rights reserved.

ISBN: 979-8-9916018-0-1

First Printing: 2024

No part of this book may be reproduced in any form whatsoever without permission in writing from the author, except by a reviewer, who may quote brief passages in critical articles or reviews.

All characters are fictional, and events portrayed in this novel are either products of the authors' imagination or used fictionally. In some cases, real names and places are used, but any resemblance to actual events, organizations or persons, living or dead, is entirely coincidence or artistic license for entertainment purposes only.

Published by
Kubo Press Works
Santa Fe, NM

Cover photo by Elaine Koyama

To contact the author: **Elaine@elainekoyama.com**

Order copies: **IngramSparks** or **KuboPressWorks@gmail.com**

Dedication

To Bill, who held my hand on my journey through grief, and helped me to the other side; and to his sister Suzanne, who brainstormed this story as we walked the Bayfield Memorial Park path on a warm summer evening.

Back to Bayfield

CONTENTS

PROLOGUE 1
CHAPTER 1 3
CHAPTER 2 13
CHAPTER 3 17
CHAPTER 4 21
CHAPTER 5 23
CHAPTER 6 29
CHAPTER 7 35
CHAPTER 8 39
CHAPTER 9 43
CHAPTER 10 49
CHAPTER 11 53
CHAPTER 12 63
CHAPTER 13 65
CHAPTER 14 71
CHAPTER 15 77
CHAPTER 16 83
CHAPTER 17 85
CHAPTER 18 87
CHAPTER 19 93
CHAPTER 20 101
CHAPTER 21 103
CHAPTER 22 107
CHAPTER 23 115

CHAPTER 24	121
CHAPTER 25	123
CHAPTER 26	129
CHAPTER 27	137
CHAPTER 28	145
CHAPTER 29	147
CHAPTER 30	149
CHAPTER 31	153
CHAPTER 32	155
CHAPTER 33	157
CHAPTER 34	163
CHAPTER 35	167
CHAPTER 36	169
CHAPTER 37	171
EPILOGUE	173
ACKNOWLEDGEMENTS	174
OTHER BOOKS BY ELAINE KOYAMA	175
BETWEEN TWO FREEDOMS	177

Back to Bayfield

Back to Bayfield

Prologue

Taylor rolled onto her back. She threw her right arm over her closed eyes blocking out the bright sunlight, the left hand reaching out, feeling for… she didn't know what. She thought she might be on Bill's boat; there was a strange rocking in the room. Her head was throbbing, and she was dreadfully thirsty. Then she heard voices downstairs. *Ah, downstairs. So I am not on a sailboat, I can eliminate that possible outcome.*

She could make out Kent's voice. She felt the bedcovers. It had the ruffles of her own bed. *Thank God. How did I get here? Who's downstairs? Kent and Sue? Kent and Jack? Chris and Kent?* Then her worst fears were realized. She heard the distinctive sound of Bill's voice intermingled with Kent's, and then she realized Sue's voice was also in the mix.

How in the world did I get to this point, she wondered.

Back to Bayfield

Chapter 1

Three years earlier, Taylor Clarke, her sunny blonde hair glistening in the spring sunlight, put the Schlage key into the old lock of the Apostles Creamery Store and at the same time took a deep breath. She had come full circle, entering the shop she had started working in as a child under the careful eye of her Grandmother Emmy, who was long buried in the cemetery on the edge of Bayfield. The new branding was coming this week—she was expanding the store, taking the sales and marketing experience she had gained as a merchandising manager at Target Corporate headquarters in Minneapolis to her hometown of Bayfield, Wisconsin.

Taylor had worked for Target for 15 years and had met her husband Mike there. He had managed the merchandise for the electronics department while she focused on developing the grocery division. They met early in their careers at a new hire happy hour. Their courtship included long walks around the Lake of the Isles, biking the city's trails, and a small wedding at the Minneapolis Woman's Club off Loring Park. They had been married for over ten years, just on the cusp of starting a family when she got the call that he had crashed his car in Palo Alto, California on a buying trip visiting high-tech companies on the leading edge of development. Her world had come crashing down. She had stayed in Minneapolis at her job; Target human resources worked with her in the months following the accident, helping her through the grief. The company had been generous, understanding, and offered counselling and time off whenever she needed. After two years, she had decided the memories of her husband and his connection to Target weighed too heavily on her mind every day and going home seemed like the right thing to do.

On a bleak, overcast day at the end of March, she loaded up her Lexus SUV with the worldly goods she hadn't sold, and began the four-hour drive north to Bayfield. She was on her way to comfort, familiarity, and a community she knew she could navigate.

The first person she ran into when she got back was Chris Kigan, the quarterback from her high school football team and who now ran the family dairy. As she walked down Rittenhouse Avenue towards the marina, her Yeti thermos coffee mug from the farm in hand, Chris came out of the Java Jolt Coffee shop, and they almost collided on the sidewalk.

"Sorry!" She exclaimed.

"Pardon, me," he said at the same time. Then they looked at each other, and the recognition bubbled up.

"Taylor!" Chris cried.

"Oh! Chris! I'd know you anywhere. How are you?" Taylor asked. She looked him over casually, but not too casually. She couldn't help but notice his broad shoulders, his blond hair--mentally noting that it was still early spring, and it was already sun bleached--and his two-day old beard that was a shade of reddish blonde. He was aging well.

She smoothed down her Patagonia windbreaker, wondering whether she had gotten the jelly stain out of the front that had dripped from her breakfast English Muffin, but then she tossed the thought aside. *This is Chris Kigan, for god's sake. He was hot in high school maybe, but we're adults now. A lot of water has gone under this bridge, and his, too, I would imagine…*

Taylor had her coffee in her hand, and Chris took her arm and led her to one of the benches on the street. "Here, let me help you, Taylor," he said quietly. "Do you have a minute to catch up? I'm doing deliveries, but I've got some time."

Chris had always been a kind and gentle soul, and he hadn't changed a bit. Taylor surmised this gentleness came from working with the dairy cows, having to milk morning and night, soothing the cows as they provided the milk for the farm and ultimately for the community. Chris had been a part of the milking operation forever, and his strong and sinewy forearms told the story of working with hundreds of cows over the past years. They sat in the sunshine of Bayfield and caught up on their lives; she in Minneapolis, he in the community they had grown up in.

Their conversation went from her work at Target, glossing over the tragic part, to how Chris was managing the farm. "I've quit milking cows the traditional way," he offered. "I know I still may look like a dairy farmer, but now the cows kinda milk themselves. We have a milking barn that they walk into, the ear tag has a chip that gets read by the scanner, and the milkers clasp onto the cows so that they can get milked anytime they feel the need. We can track every cow down to the minute they last went through the dairy barn, and when they are done giving us their bounty, we give them sweetened feed as a treat. It's really cool. I'll show the system to you sometime.

"I know it seems kinda silly to be so worked up over milking cows, but…" Chris's voice trailed off, his cheeks red from a blush of embarrassment.

"No, really, it's interesting, and I know you love it, so that's what matters. I am sure your day flies by, doing something you love," Taylor said. "I envy you, to have found your special niche in this world of ours. I'm still searching."

"Well, I guess I better get going. I can't use the line, 'The cows won't milk themselves,' anymore. I'll have to think of something else," Chris said, chuckling self-deprecatingly.

Taylor stood up first. "Thanks, Chris, It's so good to see you. I was just in town to check on some orders for Kent for later in the month. I know I'll see you more. Take care!"

"Yeah, let Kent know that I'll be mentioning him to some of my clients on the north side of Highway 13, so there might be some additional demand from there," he said. He was always thinking of others. Always so kind.

"Thanks, Chris, I'll let Kent know," She waved and turned down the hill. Chris's eyes followed her, and then he turned to get into his red pick-up with the Kigan Dairy logo on the side.

Taylor had arrived in Bayfield in early March and drove to her childhood home on the hill above town. Clarke Orchard and Country Store had been one of the stalwarts of the Bayfield Apple Festival for years. Her parents had begun the farm, and when they passed away her brother Kent took over. Kent was older than Taylor by almost 10 years, and had a fatherly disposition about him, even though he never married. If you didn't find him at the farm, you could find him at Morty's Pub on Rittenhouse Avenue, with a beer and bologna sandwich in front of him.

After she had moved back to Bayfield, Taylor moved into her old bedroom, the frilly bedspread and antique dresser still housing the clothes she had left behind. The first night she slept like a baby, waking to the smell of bacon, toast, eggs and coffee. She came downstairs to find Kent with an apron over his bib overalls and flannel plaid shirt, flipping the eggs just right to make a runny yoke, over-easy delicacy.

The first days and weeks she helped Kent out with the spring farm work, but it quickly became clear she was more overhead than help. About then Kent gave her the nudge she needed.

"How are you feeling, Taylor, about being back and getting settled?" Kent asked sympathetically one morning at breakfast.

"Kent, I love how you've been so understanding. It's been great getting back to the farm work and prepping the berry patches for the summer, but I know you don't need me. I appreciate everything you've been doing, but I realize I have to move on… I just don't know what to do, you know? I just feel lost…"

"Well, since Covid, a lot of stores have closed downtown. Gramma Emmy's store on Rittenhouse is vacant, maybe it's time for it to come back to life again. Would you be interested?" Kent prodded.

And that's how Bayfield Cool Creams and Berries began at 104 Rittenhouse Avenue. At Target, Taylor had learned how to put together a business plan and how to pitch her plans to management. She put that knowledge to work at the Bayfield Bremer Bank on Broad Street to get a business operating loan and line of credit. She had substantial savings from her job in Minneapolis, and a life insurance policy from her husband. The Covid recovery program backed her, too. She had her Gramma Emmy's recipes and processes for churned butter, ice cream and specialty whipped creams, and with Kent's berry farm, Taylor could make and sell jellies and jams. When she was growing up her grandmother would take whipped cream and add flavors—chocolate, strawberry, blueberry, and raspberry. It was a lighter alternative to ice cream, which she also handmade. On a buying trip to California, she had been introduced to taiyaki at a Japanese waffle store. She loved the smell, taste and texture of the fish shaped cone so she bought a waffle iron-like griddle to make the cones, the gaping mouth filled with whipped or ice cream. She planned on calling it the Bayfield Large-mouthed Bass.

At the same time, she bought waffle griddles that made flat fish shaped waffles that could be filled with chocolate, Oreo cookie crumbs, or custard that she named 'Bass Waffles'. They would be a new item in the town, fitting in with the commercial fishing industry that had been the mainstay in the community. With her link to Chris Kigan, she had a steady supply of milk, and Kigan's already had a grand reputation for their own line of ice cream. She struck a deal with Chris to carry his ice cream at the shop; she would make flavored soft serve to use in the taiyaki, and then she set up local suppliers of jellies and jams for this first season.

The storefront had very little repairing or retrofitting needed to be operational. Rick, the local fix-it man, tore down the old signage, pulled off the leftover décor and sanded, painted, and finally put up the new placard on the front of the shop announcing Cool Creams and Berries. Rick made Taylor's business a priority. He was a fifty-something, reddish-blond, weather-beaten, wiry man, tool belt always on, ready to work on plumbing, electrical or general refurbishing on houses, marine engines or motor bikes. Rick was the most popular guy in town, and also the go-to guy if you wanted to know the latest gossip since he was in everyone's boat or backyard working on their latest projects.

Taylor and Rick worked side-by-side—Taylor helping with finishing work, Rick working on the major changes. He put in special touches in some of the cabinets, adding shelving or pull-out racks. One afternoon, Rick turned to Taylor and asked, "Do you think you might need to stay here some nights? I could work on fixing the upstairs into a small apartment for you."

"Could you?" Taylor asked. "That would be great! I know I'll have some long days during the summer, and being able to just collapse on a bed would be so welcomed."

So, with that and a couple extra days of work, the apartment above the shop came to fruition.

When the last nail was pounded, and the last trash bag of plaster and wood scraps tossed into the bin, Rick and Taylor sat together at one of the vintage ice cream tables and parlor chairs, a cold beer in front of each of them.

"Your work is top-notch, Rick. I can't thank you enough. And I appreciate the extras that you've done. The pull out shelves are going to be a life-saver," Taylor said, surveying the room before her.

"We all want you to be successful, Taylor. And it's great to have you back in town. You know you can count on me," Rick replied. "Our families have been here a long time. We take care of each other, Right?" and he took a long swig of his Bent Paddle beer.

"You're right about that. I can't believe how much encouragement I've gotten since coming back. It's good to be home," Taylor said. "Here's to being back in Bayfield!" She raised her beer to Rick, and they clinked their bottles together in a toast.

In less than a month with Rick's help, Taylor was open for business.

It was early in the tourist season. The streets of Bayfield were quiet. Historically a fishing and lumber town, today the tourist industry kept the village of 600 people afloat. The main street, Rittenhouse, ran east/west, right into Lake Superior. Small wooden and brick storefronts lined Rittenhouse Avenue.and the adjacent streets.

Bayfield was the launch pad for the Apostle Islands National Lakeshore and neighboring Madeline Island. The Apostles consists of an archipelago off the tip of Bayfield Peninsula--a splattering of 22 islands in the pristine waters of Lake Superior. Boating among the sheltered coves and channels of the islands, and the arts, music, orchards and shopping in the area made the islands and Bayfield consistently a summer vacation destination.

The winters were notoriously severe, the waters separating Madeline Island from the Mainland freezing over so that cars and trucks travelled over the ice roads with supplies and school children who attended the Bayfield schools. Other islands were mostly uninhabited, accessible only by water, sometimes by ice, with campgrounds and hiking paths. Visitors who didn't have their own watercraft depended on the thriving ferry and boat taxi business to get to the remote islands.

The cool winds off Lake Superior brought visitors from points south to escape the heavy, humid heat of the summer. Lake Superior, on the border of Canada and known to be the coldest and deepest of the Great Lakes, was a natural air conditioner.

Back to Bayfield

Chapter 2

The days began to take on a shape and rhythm that centered Taylor. She continued to live with Kent at the family berry farm, helping him when needed, but early spring was a time for the bushes and trees to flower in anticipation of the strawberries, raspberries, blueberries and apples to follow. There wasn't much work to be done there.

Her shop in town began to draw customers, but the season was beginning slowly. Unseasonably cool weather discouraged tourists, and the few tourists that wandered in weren't too interested in ice cream. She hung her shingle out and began dropping off brochures announcing her business to the local tourist information centers. She travelled to the buying show at the Minneapolis Convention Center and began building a small inventory of tourist swag. All she needed were a few warm weekends to jumpstart the traffic through the store.

Chris Kigan stopped in daily to check on her supply of milk for butter, ice and whipped cream. Each day she would wake at 4:30 am to churn the day's supply of Emmy's Cool Creams butter and refresh the tubs of whipped creams and ice creams.

Early on a Saturday morning, Sue Boyt stopped in. She was the local high school guidance counsellor, summertime Chamber of Commerce front desk lady, and Bayfield mayor. She seemed to have been too busy running the community to fall in love and get married, so in addition to all the other roles she had, she was also the local spinster, master gardener and go-to go-getter for getting anything done. She opened the door to the Cool Creams and Berries shop and the sweet tinkling tones of the doorbell announced her entry.

"Good morning! Anybody home?" she called out.

Taylor came out of the back kitchen, wiping her hands on a cotton tea towel, a bit of whipped cream on her cheek, strands of hair wet from sweat poking out from her headband. She recognized Sue immediately and said, "Oh, Hi there, Sue! How are you this morning? Anything I can do for you?"

"Well, yes you can. We could use you as a business owner to get involved in the Chamber. You need business, we promote business, you give and you'll get, got me? Our meetings are short and sweet. We could use your skills for sure.

"As a first step, the Chamber has some window posters that I'd like to put up. Can I get your permission to post the Memorial Day Season Kick-Off events calendar in your window? There's a dance at the Bayfield Yacht Club. You should come!" She said all this without taking a breath.

"Sue, of course you can put the calendar in the window, but I doubt that I will go to any dances. I'm thinking my dancing days are over." Taylor said, somewhat diffidently. The door opened again, the bell sounding the entrance of Chris Kigan.

"What's this I am overhearing?" Chris asked as he walked in with the cream bucket. "You're thinking you're not going to the Memorial Day

Dance? I'm going, so why don't you come with me? We can relive Homecoming all over again," he said smiling.

"No reliving anything for me," Taylor said, smiling back. "But if you're going, maybe I'll go, too. But I think I'll talk Kent into going with me. I hate to leave him home alone."

"OK, no problem. I'll see you there, anyway," Chris replied. "No high school relapses, either." He smiled wryly. Taylor patted him on the shoulder playfully.

He set the cannister on the counter, and the two women watched him walk back out the door, his broad shoulders filling out the flannel plaid shirt under the jeans jacket. "He's a really nice guy," Sue commented.

"Yeah, no question about that," Taylor replied. "I've always kinda liked him. He's as gentle as those cows that he spends so much time with. And I mean that in a really good way."

"Oh, I understand. Totally." Then Sue changed tack. "By the way, I know you start really early, and you usually have to deliver Cool Creams back to the berry farm after the batch is done. I head that way every day after my morning business. Would you like me to run that out to your brother on my way? It would save you a trip."

"Why, Sue, that would be great, especially on the weekends. It gets so busy, and sometimes I don't feel like I have time even for that short run. It would really help out. Thanks!"

"And if I have weekend time, I'd be happy to help here at the shop. It's fun for me to keep busy, if it's ok with you?" Sue said, her voice going up into the question at the end.

"It's not only OK with me, it's totally all right with me. But I gotta tell you, I won't be able to pay you right now. Funds are tight, and I don't have enough to hire you…" Taylor countered.

"No problem. When you get on your feet, we can make it right. It's important for the town to see you successful," Sue replied, ever the city mayor, chamber member, and cheerleader.

Chapter 3

The wind was coming out of the northwest at a nice, steady 15 knots on May 31, filling the sails of the HMS Loon as it honed in on the Outer Island lighthouse. The sloop then veered to the portside of Outer, and then there was the visual of Stockton Island Presque Isle Point. Bill Boyt stood at the helm, focused forward, his eyes and his mind miles ahead of the bow of the boat.

Bill had left Bayfield right out of high school, and seldom came back. He was one of the only Bayfield kids to get accepted at, let alone attend, Stanford. After finishing his undergraduate degree in economics, he returned to the Midwest, but not to Bayfield. He landed in Chicago, where he worked in the banking industry for a spell, then got his MBA from the University of Chicago. His specialty was internet marketing, before internet marketing was a thing. Making money was fast and furious in the internet space, and Bill took advantage of the opportunities his background and his education gave him. He cut a wide swath in the Chicago business circle and became a benefactor of the arts community there. He met the daughter of the president of the Chicago Board of Trade while in graduate school, married her within a year, and rode the wave of Chicago society. He fit well into that league—tall, with dark almost black hair and clear hazel-blue eyes, coupled with a long, lean, athletic physique. He looked more tennis player than football jock. Dressed in the bow tie and tux that evening events required of him, he cut an imposing yet supporting figure alongside his glittering socialite of a wife.

Right that morning he was sailing towards his past, a past that he never thought he would return to after his parents died. His life had been one phenomenal event after another, right up until he found his drop-dead gorgeous wife in bed with one of his backgammon playing friends. Or more precisely, ex-friend. That had been two years ago, and the pain of that discovery was still intense. To alleviate his guilt and to help with the recovery, his ex-father-in-law gave him the HMS Loon, and he began sailing the sloop that had spent too many days docked at the CYC, Chicago Yacht Club. The Loon was a classic low-profile sailboat. It came out of the era when teakwood was used generously both inside and out, giving the craft a feel of old money. The owners knew that most of the moving parts had already been replaced multiple times, and that only the deep pockets of the Chicago wealthy kept it in top sailing shape.

The sole family Bill had left in Bayfield was his older sister Sue. His parents had sold their interests in the Weyerhaeuser Lumber Company and had remained in Bayfield in their retirement. Sue lived in the cottage across the street from their parents' rambling Queen Anne style mansion where he and Sue had grown up, but since their parents' death the main house had remained vacant and had fallen into disrepair.

Sue had no interest in living in the big, drafty mansion, and since she was single with no kids, had no need for the five bedrooms and four baths. She was happiest in her cottage, with its tour-worthy butterfly garden, and more modest view of Lake Superior. Her energy was spent on the community where it was needed and appreciated. With an intellect as sharp as her younger brother's, she knew what she wanted and went after it. With a significant age gap between them, they both pursued their disparate dreams in different ways.

Bill was sailing the Loon from the Chicago Yacht Club to Bayfield with one mate, Paul, a quiet man a few years younger. In the two years since his marriage broke up, Bill had sailed the Loon in the Club race from Chicago to Mackinac Island twice, both times coming in among the top five finishers in his class. Those races required a full crew. But his intent on this trip was to spend some much-needed time alone, to reflect upon the past and plan for the future. Bill was particular in whose company he kept, and Paul's ability to seemingly disappear made him the perfect companion for this trip home. He was easy-going, kept to himself, and had an uncanny sensitivity, understanding Bill's need for quiet solitude. Bill appreciated the privacy Paul extended towards him and often their relationship was more peer-to-peer than employer/employee.

The Loon sailed by Presque Isle Point and followed the North Channel towards Bayfield, passing Hermit and Basswood Islands on the starboard side, and the length of Madeline Island on the portside.

Soon his parents' home came into view. The stately house had a round, three-story tower facing the lake and two small dormers on the south side of the third floor, with a wrap-around porch on the first level. White pillars were spaced evenly around the porch. The house sat just down the street from Holy Family Catholic Church whose steeple was visible for miles. The home was unmistakable. Striking. And from a distance, the rotting wood, missing shingles, and broken porch boards were undetectable. He could see Sue's blue-green, two-storied home just south and down the hill.

Watching for the Madeline Island ferries, Bill turned into the Northwest wind, started the engine, and with Paul's help, dropped his mainsail, and furled the jib. He turned the Loon back toward Bayfield and sailed into the marina where he had reserved a dock space and where he was planning to spend the next few weeks while he readied his parents' home for sale.

Chapter 4

Sue Boyt checked her watch, waiting for Kent to arrive and take the freshly churned butter she had brought from Cool Creams. She knew from her last contact with Bill that he would be pulling into the marina anytime now, and she wanted to be there to meet him at the dock.

Clarke Orchards had a small retail storefront on the farm and Kent kept it stocked with a few items that supported his berry and apple business. When the berries came in, he counted on U-Pick sales to add icing to the usual skinny profit margins. His plan was to sell a bit of Emmy's Butter from Taylor's store, but it was mostly there to build awareness of the Bayfield Cool Creams and Berries shop. He kept the retail business for the occasional shopper but liked to direct them to the main street of Bayfield to spend most of their tourist dollars.

Sue was ready to leave the butter on the counter when Kent rounded the corner of the storage shed and saw her Chevy Tahoe. He took the stairs two at a time to where Sue waited, a look of happiness on his face.

"Sue! Sorry to keep you waiting. Forgot that you were coming, and here I am, making you wait. That's no way to impress a girl, now, is it?" She knew it was a rhetorical question. She and Kent had been classmates and friends since grade school, and they knew each other as well as any old friends might.

"No worries. I was just about ready to leave. I heard from Bill; he's heading our way in the Loon. Should be here any second, so I gotta run.

Just checking to see if you were going to be coming to town tonight?" she asked hopefully, though her blank expression was more like how she would talk to the clerk at Andy's Groceries.

"Now, I hadn't given it much thought, but maybe I will. This is the Memorial Day dance at the Yacht Club, right? Jack mentioned it to me when he stopped by on his way to church yesterday. I reckon I better go, make sure nothing un-toward happens, you know?" he said this with a twinkle in his eye.

Sue let his comment slide. "I'm hoping Bill will go, but he's been in a blue funk since that little hussy of a wife wandered out of the pasture. Why any woman would wander on Bill, I'll never understand, but I guess that's why I don't live in the big city. So, I'll see you there, will I?" She asked Kent again.

"Well, like I said, I figure I'll be going, though dancing isn't my thing." He shrugged and looked out onto the fields across the road. "You best be headed back to town if you want to meet up with that brother of yours. I'll see you tonight."

Sue turned to go, and then tossed over her shoulder, "And Kent, maybe wear something other than those blue overalls. There will be summer people showing up, you know." She paused awkwardly, then continued, "You wouldn't want to embarrass Taylor, now, would you?"

"No ma'am," Kent said with a small salute.

Sue kept walking towards her Tahoe, a slow blush tinging her cheeks pink.

Chapter 5

Sue parked in the marina lot and walked towards the docks, her eyes scanning the bay for a moving mast that would indicate a sailboat within the protected waters. Jimmy, the marina all-purpose dock hand, greeted her and calmed her anxiety. "No, that Mr. Bill hasn't come in yet. We had radio contact when he was at Basswood Island about 20 minutes ago. You have plenty of time, Miss Sue." Jimmy called everyone Mister or Miss, or Missus, depending on his familiarity. Everyone just called him Jimmy.

Sue walked along the top of the breaker wall towards the entrance of the marina. As she held her hand up to shield her eyes from the bright sunlight, she saw the Loon slowly approaching. She waved towards the boat, and she heard a short horn reply. Her brother was coming home at last.

As Bill pulled the Loon into the Bayfield Marina, he cut back the engine to enter slowly. He had been given H3, a dockside mooring parallel to the Bayfield walking path. He knew these were the prime spots for show—anyone walking along the shore saw the length of the boats on H dock. He made a mental note to thank the marina office, since he knew those spots were at a premium. As he rounded the length of dock C, he saw Sue standing at H3 prepared to catch the bow line. Paul was up, had put the fenders out and was ready to throw the line to Sue. As Bill brought the Loon around, the crew manned their posts—Paul flipped the bow line to Sue; she looped it over the dock cleat, moved to the stern, where he handed the line to Sue, and she secured the back of the boat to the dock cleat. Paul nimbly hopped to the dock, the midship line in hand and secured the final line to the dock cleat. Bill cut the engine, climbed out to the dock and gave Sue a big hug.

Paul continued securing the boat, then waved them off. "I can take it from here, sir," he said to Bill. "You go enjoy yourself. I'll introduce myself to the marina crew and then go get a late lunch. I'll be fine."

Bill acknowledged the offer and turned his attention to Sue. "Where should we go have lunch?" he asked.

Sue, ever prepared, said, "I made a reservation for the rooftop at the Bayfield Inn. You can watch both the downtown and marina activity while we talk."

"Sounds great, sis. I'm starved. Let's go!"

And they continued down the dock, Bill draping an arm affectionately over his sister's shoulder.

That same day, Jack, Kent's best friend, stopped at Morty's Pub and ran into Kent having a fried bologna sandwich and a New Glaris Spotted Cow beer for lunch. Jack sat down next to Kent at the bar, and before he could say, "I'll have my regular," Moira plopped a Leinie in front of him.

"That's why I keep coming in here," Jack said. "You all are mind-readers."

"If that's mind-reading, then I'm a downright genius, eh?" chuckled Kent. "But I'm no mind-reader. What are you up to, Jack?"

"Well, I was thinking," Jack started.

"Hey, everyone! Jack's been thinking! Beers on the house! He's paying!" Kent yelled out.

"Now just a doggone minute, you're spending my money pretty easily, don't you think?" Jack said to Kent. Then he said to the handful of guys in the bar, "Buy your own beer, mates. I'll be buying when I find me that young filly to get hitched to." There was general laughter.

"Means you won't ever be paying, eh, Jack?" one of the patrons ventured to say.

Jack turned to Kent and asked him if Sue had asked if he was going to the dance. Kent looked intensely into his bologna. "Well, she might have mentioned it this morning when I was coming in from doing chores, yeah," he responded. "How about you?" he countered.

"Well, no, not directly, but she kinda hinted that it was a big event. I don't think she should go alone; I was thinking one of us should drive her, what do you think?" Jack said as he studied his beer and picked at the label.

"Yeah, that might be nice. A lady shouldn't be out late at night alone, I suppose," Kent said.

"OK, well, maybe I'll call her and see," Jack said, then turned to Moira and called out, "Hey, Moira, you got a phone book?"

Moira turned and said incredulously, "What's a phonebook?"

"Kent continued to study his bologna and said, "822-4224."

Jack pulled his focus down to his friend's face. "What? What's that? That's Sue's number?"

"Well, ya, it's pretty easy to remember—822-4224. Not that I call it or anything," Kent said to his sandwich.

Jack smiled at his friend, put his hand on Kent's shoulder and said, "Well, anybody that knows a woman's phone number by heart should put it to good use. You call her, see if she wants a ride. I mean, it's not a proposal. It's just a ride, after all, buddy."

Taylor debated all day about calling Chris Kigan back and offering to go with him to the dance, but the more she thought about it, the more she felt like he had offered just to be nice. And she didn't want Kent to have to go alone. Kent was the perfect excuse and the perfect escort. She had been widowed for almost three years, and even now missed having that dedicated partner to go out with. As she was finishing a batch of strawberry ice cream, the bells above her door rang, announcing a visitor. She peered out and saw Sue walking slowly towards her.

"Hey! What's up, Sue?" Taylor asked. Sue was picking at a piece of lint on her sweater.

"What? No, nothing. Nothing's up. I was just wondering what you were going to wear tonight." She mumbled. "To the dance, I mean…"

"Gee, I hadn't really thought about it much. It will mostly be locals, so I don't think it much matters. I suppose there'll be some of the tourist crowd, though. Why?" Taylor said. She thought it strange for Sue to be going down this path. Neither woman was a fashion maven, and mostly wore jeans and a T. "I don't think Kent will worry much how I look, anyway. I'm going to tag along with him to the dance, I figure."

Sue got a worried look in her eyes. "Before I forget to tell you, Bill's back in town. He just sailed in from Chicago.

There was a pause.

"You're going to go with Kent? I guess that's ok, it's just a bit awkward..." Sue's voice trailed off.

"Awkward? Why? We go lots of places together; I don't think this is any diff... Hey what's going on here? Sue, is there something I don't know?" Taylor faced Sue head on.

"Ah, well, I just got a call from Kent and he asked if I wanted a ride to the dance tonight. I said, sure, so I guess if you go too, there will be three of us going... And of course, that's fine, it's just a ride," Sue finished lamely. "I wouldn't mind," she said just for good measure.

"Oh, Sue, that's so nice! And of course I wouldn't make a third. I mean I'm single, but I'm not desperate. I'll call Chris and catch a ride with him. Or I can drive here to the shop and walk, it's only three blocks or so. It's no big deal. And I might stay in the apartment above the shop tonight, anyway, you know, just in case you might want to go back to the farm later..." Taylor offered, awkwardly.

Sue looked at Taylor with a horrified look on her face. "OMG, what are you thinking, girl? I'm just getting a ride with your brother; I'm not marrying him!" And she turned abruptly and stomped out the door.

Geez, Louise, thought Taylor. *I wonder what's up with that.*

And then she realized that Sue had dropped another bombshell. Bill was back in town. Bill, who had been her nemesis since first grade, when they competed in every subject and on every test to see who could do better. In sixth grade, the year she sat right in front of him, she had beaten him in an arm-wrestling contest, but he had been the one chosen to dissect the cow's eye.

They were competitors, good friends, and she had harbored a crush that she could never shake. Bill and Chris had been best friends and competitors in school, too. While Chris didn't have the book-smarts, he had the brawn and the practical knowledge that comes with farming; and he had the heart that sometimes Taylor thought Bill lacked. She had ended up being the valedictorian and Bill was the salutatorian of their class. She had gone to UW Madison, and he had gone to Stanford—he had family money, she had the scholarship. She had pretty much tried to lose track of Bill since they graduated, but his internet success made him the topic of local gossip and someone she couldn't fully forget.

Bill. She had tried not to think of him for so long. The crush that had started in elementary school never dissipated, and had lasted until they graduated.

Then her thoughts flew to Kent. And Sue. *Wow,* she paused in her thinking.

Yep, she thought. *I think I better park my car at the shop and walk to the dance. It would be better to walk back alone and better to leave the berry farm open to other opportunities.*

Chapter 6

Memorial Day in Bayfield is on the cusp of the seasons—the temperatures can range from the 40s to the 80s. This year it sat in the middle, nights dropped into the 50s and daytime temperatures were in the 70s. But with blue painted skies, sun warming the air, and the green of hardwoods mixed with evergreen trees blanketing the hillsides, the weather felt perfect.

Taylor drove into town from the orchard wearing a pale peach, cap-sleeved dress with a flowing skirt that hit her just above the ankles. She threw on an old sweater she found in her closet from her youth, and with ballerina-styled flats, she looked both youthful and playful. She had traded her Lexus for a used blue Ford F-150 Crew Cab for business and that was the vehicle she drove into town. She parked in the back of the building and ran her overnight bag up the stairs to the apartment above the business. The space was sparse, some of it used as an office for the bookkeeping, but it also had a small kitchen, living area and bedroom.

The dance started at 7, and it was already 7. She toyed with her hair, twisting it one way, and then the other, trying clips and barrettes to keep it in place, and then finally gave up and let it down around her shoulders.

She left through the front door of the shop, turned right onto Rittenhouse Avenue, then turned right again at South 1st Street. It was a two-block walk to the Bayfield Yacht Club, easy on a beautiful evening in Bayfield, where most everything in town was within walking distance.

As she walked past the Bayfield Maritime Museum, she looked to her left at the docks in the marina and saw the HMS Loon moored front and center. It was a lovely boat, a good 36 feet long, she was guessing. *Long enough,* she thought. The Yacht Club was housed in an unassuming building between the Marina Park and Playground and a couple working slips. The dance committee had cleared out the main room and opened the garage door that faced the street, and the party had already spilled out onto the asphalt and to the Marina Park picnic shelter. The music was pouring out of the building.

A large group had already gathered, and as she walked past the fountain sculpture, Kent and Sue drove by. She waved, they waved back, and then she was at the dance.

As she walked up to the open garage door at the front of the building, she saw Chris talking to Rick and Jimmy. Then she noticed a man she didn't recognize in the group of three men. She walked up to Chris.

Chris, always the gentleman, moved so the circle of men got bigger to include her. She smiled at Rick and Jimmy, and then looked at the new guy. "Hi, I'm Taylor. I'm afraid I don't know you, yet…" she said, checking out the stranger.

Jimmy quickly jumped in and introduced her. "Taylor, this is Paul, he sailed with Bill Boyt from Chicago. Paul, Taylor Clarke, local businesswoman and friend of ours."

Paul was a trim, fit man, younger than Taylor. He had short curly hair, dark smiling eyes and appeared to be African American. Taylor extended her hand, and felt his strong, calloused hand grip hers. "My pleasure, Miss Clarke. Paul Frazer, at your service," he said.

She felt like she had stepped back in time. "Paul, the pleasure is all mine. We need some fresh faces here in Bayfield, as you will find out. I'd guess you'll be a popular guy here in town in no time," Taylor said good naturedly. "Please come to my shop soon. I run Bayfield Cool Creams and Berries on Rittenhouse.

"You sailed here with Bill Boyt, I understand," she said more as a statement than a question.

"Yes, ma'am, I did. Mr. Boyt was still on the boat when I left to come here. I believe he is staying on board during our stay," Paul offered.

She saw out of the corner of her eye Sue and Kent walking in, Sue walking in front, Kent following. Across the room, Jack was also watching the two of them arrive.

The music was an eclectic mix of country western, 60s/70s/80s and current pop rock. Chris offered to get Taylor a drink. He asked, "Taylor, what are you drinking nowadays? You still a sloe gin screwdriver drinker?"

Taylor blushed. "No, no more of that stuff. One night during college I had one too many, and I have NEVER had another one. But I do like gin. I'll have a gin and tonic, if you don't mind."

Chris moved to the makeshift bar, and Taylor turned to Rick to ask him about his availability for some additional carpentry work at the shop. His back was to the garage door, so when she turned to talk to him, she was facing the garage door entrance. That's when she saw Bill walking up to the Club.

Coincidentally, a Carly Simon song began, *You're So Vain*. No kidding.

Just then Chris came back with her gin and tonic. She thanked him warmly, swallowed the drink in one grateful gulp, sat her glass on a nearby high top and wrapped her arm around his neck. "Let's dance," she said. And he led her onto the dance floor.

The gin and tonic that Chris got her was just the first of several. Taylor hadn't been to a small-town dance in forever. She was missing the safety of her husband, she was single, there was no one in the world that she wanted to see less than Bill Boyt. He had broken her heart when they graduated. He had tossed her aside like a used coffee pod. He had to go off to the fancy college. She had to stay in Wisconsin. She had always been smarter, worked harder, tried her best. And he jetted off--or drove off, or whatever he did back after graduation--to go to school on the West Coast, far from home, far from her.

She danced with Chris, and then with Rick, then with Jimmy, then with Kent, who took her aside, gave her a plate of chips and dip, and asked her what was going on. This was after the fourth or fifth drink.

"OK, little sister, what's going on? This isn't like you, and you know it," he said as kindly and quietly as he could.

"I'm OK, I'm OK. I'm an adult now. It's all water under the bridge. I am so over it," she said drunkenly. A 60s song by Neil Sedaka began, *Breakin' Up is Hard to Do*. Taylor looked at Kent with a clear eye. "He dumped me to go to Stanford. OK, I know we didn't even date that much in school, but even so, he must have known I liked him. He never came back. He never gave me the time of day. I am so over it," she said clearly.

Kent just looked at her with a slight frown. "Clearly not," was all he said.

In a small town at a local dance, it is impossible to avoid a person for too long. That was the case for Taylor and the Memorial Day Dance. As the dance progressed, and dancers expanded the dance floor to the parking lot asphalt, Bill and Taylor finally came face to face.

"Well, Bill. Fancy that we would meet here. And wouldn't you know, you're also the best dancer here. Is there anything you can't do?" Taylor asked sarcastically.

"I'd be the first to say I can't do a multitude of things. How are you, Taylor? Or maybe tonight isn't the best time to ask you that... Because obviously you are having a good time, if the number of dance partners is any indication. You look as lovely as ever, Taylor. It's so nice to see you," he said seemingly sincere.

"I wasn't even watching you dance, you know. I just knew you would be good at it, still. I mean, I don't even think about you anymore, you know. I was so happy before. I had the perfect husband. He was my world. I..." and then Taylor bent over and held her hand over her mouth. She stumbled and ran to the edge of the playground. Bill followed, one hand out near Taylor's back, but not touching her. She began to spew all the gin, tonic, chips and ranch dressing over the fence onto the wood chips. Bill stood beside her, his bright white handkerchief out and waiting for her next move.

Back to Bayfield

Chapter 7

And that's how she came to be lying in her childhood bed, a massive hangover and vertigo afflicting Taylor as she rolled onto her back. Then she heard the voices of Kent, Bill and Sue downstairs that had interrupted her disjointed thoughts.

She rolled out of bed, needing the bathroom. She stood up and felt a little bit of a whorl move through the room. She gripped her bed for balance and paused to let the world stop spinning. She moved tentatively out the door and down the hall to the bathroom. She realized she was still in the peach-colored dress, which looked only slightly worse for wear. She looked into the mirror and thought, *the dress looks better than I do this morning.*

She could smell coffee and what could be ham and eggs cooking in butter. She threw off her dress and pulled on the jeans and T shirt she wore the day before. A quick brush of her hair, a pull back into a ponytail, and she was as ready as she could be.

Taylor took a deep breath and said to herself, "Time to face the music."

The details were gory, and this is a family friendly story. No need to describe the embarrassment when Taylor walked into the kitchen. No way to show the questioning look in Bill's eyes when she finally raised her eyes to his. No way to recount the surprise when Taylor saw Sue put her hand on Kent's shoulder when she handed him his coffee. No words to chronicle the story of how the two sets of siblings quietly ate that breakfast of ham and eggs and toast with Emmy's butter infused in it all. No way to express the range of feelings that ran through the room. Enough to say the resentful sentiments and emotions that Taylor had felt so strongly the night before seemed like they were a lifetime ago, as they were.

Today, the day after the Memorial Day Dance, was a Tuesday, and the official start of the summer season. Bill was talking to Kent about some impeller problem that he was having on the Loon. He wanted to swap out the davits, small cranes that held the dinghy on the back of the Loon. While the Loon issues were being attended to, he and Sue had to start the monstrous task of getting their family home ready to sell. Taylor finished her breakfast in silence, as much because she didn't have anything to add to the conversation as the embarrassment she still felt. She pushed back from the table to stand up, and to her surprise, Bill rose with her. She was puzzled, as were Kent and Sue. The three of them looked at Bill, quizzically.

"New habits die hard," Bill said apologetically. Taylor then realized he had stood because she had. It had felt so old worldly, but somehow suited him so well.

"No," she said. "Don't apologize. It's rather nice. It's pretty rural here, not too many worry about manners and such. In Minneapolis, either. Maybe it's a Chicago thing." she looked out the kitchen window.

"Uh, is my truck here?" she asked. *How did I get home?* she wondered.

"Bill drove it up this morning," Sue replied. She nodded her acknowledgement. "Kent and I brought you home last night. You were in no condition to drive or walk for that matter."

"Thank you, both," she said looking pointedly at Sue and Kent. "I know I owe you."

"Bill, can I give you a lift back to town? I've got to shower and get to the shop to open. It won't take me but a few minutes," she offered. It was her olive branch.

He didn't bite. "No, thank you. I'm catching a ride with Sue. We have some business to attend to."

"OK, whatever," Taylor said as she turned around and headed up the stairs.

Back to Bayfield

Chapter 8

The summer began in earnest after Memorial Day and business picked up every week. Taylor's Bayfield Large-mouth Bass cone was a great success, but the name was too much of a mouthful and soon the cone became known as a Bayfield Bass. Up and down Rittenhouse Avenue tourists would ask where they could get their Bayfield Bass, and all roads led to the Bayfield Cool Creams and Berries shop.

Plans for the Loon had been set, so work on the Boyt family home began in earnest, too. Sue had come up with home history from the Bayfield Heritage Association and found it was built by the Boutin family at the turn of the 1900s. At one-point nuns from the church next door had lived there. Rick became a fixture at the house, his construction skills in high demand. Bill began helping and doing much of the work side-by-side with Rick.

Chris Kigan was the epitome of a gentleman, and never mentioned how the dance ended for Taylor after his initial inquiry the next day about how she was feeling. Her response to his question: "Embarrassed, thank you for asking."

Paul, Bill's first mate on board, became a frequent visitor to the shop. He kept busy on the boat, repairing, painting, staining, repairing all over again. The davits and a new dinghy arrived, and he was busy putting it all together. Many times, Paul would be at the shop when Chris stopped to drop off cream. The three of them would take a break and have hot drinks from Java Jolt coffee across the street or High Winds coffee shop down the block and kitty corner from Cool Creams. A Bayfield Bass cone with or without whipped or ice cream made the perfect companion to the black coffee. Taylor used Paul and Chris as guinea pigs, testing the Bass Waffle fillings for their reactions.

The three would sit and gossip about the latest escapades happening in the small town, careful not to tread on anyone's current or past passions, which primarily meant they didn't talk about Bill. Sue was a drop-in helper at the shop, so she would join the coffee klatches, and Kent was often found at the shop the same time Sue was there.

Later in June, Paul, Chris and Taylor went to the Big Top Chautauqua to hear the Ozark Mountain Daredevils, the three of them taking the shuttle to avoid driving the narrow two-lane to Ski Hill Road and up the hill to the Big Top. During the evening Taylor sat next to Chris, sometimes next to Paul. Sometimes Paul sat next to Chris.

She found both men attractive, easy to be with, non-threatening. They were the perfect guy-friends. The three of them turned heads, and they knew it. Paul stood out in the Scandinavian-settled northern Wisconsin community with his dark skin, tight-curled hair, luscious lips. Chris was on the other end of the spectrum, fair-skinned, fair-haired, always suffering from sunburn on his nose or cheeks. Taylor had the good luck of being fair-haired but with skin that tanned like a Mediterranean. The three bonded early and spent easy and companionable hours together.

Bill was true to his original intent on coming back to Bayfield. The repairs on the Boyt house were coming along nicely. Delays were popping up due to lumber shortages, and the architectural shingles were back ordered for weeks. His original plan to spend only a few weeks was turning into, in all likelihood, a couple of months.

Amidst all the work, Bill had plenty of time to think through the events of the past few years and contemplate his future. He had opportunities to hook up with single women in Chicago. Aside from the high-profile breakup he had just been through, his life prior to marrying into a society family was high profile enough. He was one of the tech boom millionaires before he was thirty, and the dollars just kept multiplying. He often thought of the phrase *money makes money*. In his case, it was certainly true.

What troubled him was that the money also attracted women he wasn't much interested in. He chuckled to himself. *Tough luck, huh? I'm where most every guy wants to be, and I still want more. How is that normal?*

Many evenings Paul would be out and about. He was a much more social being than Bill. On those nights Bill would cook a lean meal for one. On the nights they were both on board, they would move about like two bachelors, making minimalist meals, retreating to one of the settees or to their cabins, a dim light to read by. Occasionally Bill would spend time after work with Sue. But Sue was busy with her own social ventures, and she made it clear that she was not her brother's keeper.

While his days were busy with repairs and boat maintenance, Bill had plenty of time to sail, too. Paul was his first mate and sailing companion, and continued to fill the role well.

For a man tortured about his future, torn about his past, and with too much time and money to think about both, sailing filled Bill's intellect with the mechanics of sailing and the calmness of being on and in the water.

As for Sue, she was focused on her next project—the July 4th celebration in Bayfield. This was the biggest event of the summer, and her days were consumed with details, details, details. She was like the captain of a tall ship, totally in command. The town was having concerts, parades, a farmers' market the Saturday before and a pig roast and fireworks on the 4th. She was also organizing a butterfly garden tour around town, showing off the many butterfly gardens that had been planted and groomed in recent years.

The summer was in full swing.

Chapter 9

Bill hiked the Big Ravine Trail that started at Washington Avenue and followed the valley all the way up the hill to where many of the orchards and berry farms that made Bayfield renowned. It wasn't far from the Clarke Orchard farm. He walked from the Loon to the Boyt big house, to the trailhead. It was a trail he had taken before, used by residents and visitors alike.

Bill enjoyed the sounds of the flowing creek, the tall maple and basswood trees filtering sunlight down to the forest floor, the birdsong made for a welcomed reprieve so close to town. He had begun to enjoy his time in Bayfield in a way he hadn't expected—the slower pace, few evening commitments and the physical labor involved not only on the house repairs, but in sailing the boat. Sailing required brawn and brains and while Bill felt he was a proficient sailor, he knew he could be better.

He was thinking of the Loon, the joy he felt when the wind filled the sails and propelled them forward, silent except for the rush of the wind. It was exhilarating to feel power without the roar of an engine. He felt the duality of the might of the wind in the sails and fragility of a single man in the vastness of the water. The walking path was narrow and steep in places. He had vistas across the ravine that ran beside him. Several hikers passed Bill as he was walking uphill and they down. Everyone greeted each other, an air of camaraderie and friendship projecting as they passed. He was working up a sweat, the warm June day combined with the humidity created by the trees reduced the evaporation of sweat.. He was thinking about how lovely the trail would be in October, the colors from the leaves of the hardwoods would be spectacular, when he looked up and almost collided with Taylor Clarke.

"Whoa, hi, there, Taylor. You caught me daydreaming. You coming from the farm?" Bill asked. He was conscious of the sweat trickling down the middle of his back, the heat radiating off his body. She looked fresh.

"Looks like you came from the bottom. You're almost there, just a little ways to go now. I did come from the farm; thought I'd take the long way into town.

"I caught a ride out with Sue. She wasn't ready to head back, so I thought I'd walk. She's been spending a lot of time at the Orchard, I wonder why," Taylor said playfully, looking at Bill carefully. She had a twinkle in her eye.

Bill checked his watch, "I didn't realize what time it was. I should head back myself. Can I join you?" he asked.

"It's a public path. Come on," Taylor replied. "Keep up."

They walked in companionable silence for a while, Taylor in the lead. She had an easy, relaxed stride. Her blond shoulder-length hair swayed with each step; her arms swung freely. Taylor was tall, but not a pencil thin woman. She was curvy in all the right places, and the way she carried herself, it was clear she was comfortable in her skin. Bill followed her down, enjoying the view.

"How's the work on the homeplace?" Taylor tossed over her shoulder.

"Yes, it's coming along," Bill replied shortly. He was breathing harder than Taylor, so his answers were brief. "We're almost done with the porch board replacements, and the shingles come later this week. Then we paint the exterior, and it should be ready to sell.

"I've never said anything to you, but I'm really sorry about your husband, Taylor. That had to be a tough loss," Bill added.

Taylor's left foot slid, and both she and Bill reached out. Bill caught her arm to steady her. "Thanks, Bill," it wasn't entirely clear whether she was referring to his helping hand or his condolences. "It was a rough year or two there for a while. My friends in the Cities were great, and so was my company. I couldn't have made it through without them."

Bill asked, "Why did you come back? It sounds like you had things back on track in Minneapolis. Even though I think Bayfield is the winner here," he added.

"Yeah, I thought I had it together in Minneapolis, and I did. Things were moving forward; I came out of that blue grief fog and work was more than satisfying. But everywhere I turned, there he was. I still needed to come to terms with that. He was never a part of Bayfield, so I figured he wouldn't be around every corner here. And I was right. He isn't hovering over me here. I'm so busy it helps, and Chris, Kent and Sue have helped me move on."

"I guess I am in the same boat in a way. Of course, I wouldn't compare getting divorced with becoming a wi—widow," he stumbled over the word, it sounded like a word for an old biddy, not this vibrant, healthy, handsome woman walking nimbly in front of him.

Taylor laughed. "Don't worry, I AM a widow, like it or not. It sounds strange, doesn't it? I mean, I never in a million years thought I'd be widowed…"

"Well, as strange as it sounds, I never imagined I'd be a divorcee, either. I was totally blindsided," he admitted. "This trip was my escape, too. Brenda didn't want me to leave—her or Chicago--but I couldn't stay with her. She was having an affair with one of the guys I played backgammon with, for god's sake. I think she would have been perfectly happy with this guy on the side, and me at her other side, but I—I just couldn't. I loved her too much. I may still love her. And I think that's why I could never share her. Call me old fashioned, but I took those wedding vows pretty seriously."

"I've always thought divorced people have it harder than widows. We get all the sympathy. I think people are always looking for who's at fault in a divorce. And the fact of the matter is, bad things just happen sometimes, don't you think?" Taylor hadn't missed a step during this long, serious chat. But now she slowed to a stop and turned so they were able to look at each other. Bill stepped forward to be beside her and so the height differential wasn't so great.

"It's, I don't know the right words, but it's nice—I mean not 'nice' but… you know what I mean. I haven't been able to talk to anyone about how I feel, how it feels to be alone and working through this predicament." Bill stumbled. Usually so eloquent, so sure with his words, he was clearly on unproven ground.

"No worries, mate," Taylor joked. "I feel your pain. You've gone through a loss just as impactful as the loss I've been through, just different." The trail had come to an end, and they had continued walking down to Rittenhouse and to Cool Creams and Berries. "You want to come in?" she asked him.

"Maybe not today. I'm meeting Jimmy and Paul to talk davits. I'll take a raincheck?" he asked hopefully.

Taylor gave Bill a quick hug. "The door's always open, friend."

Back to Bayfield

Chapter 10

The next day, when Chris made his cream delivery, not two minutes passed when the tinkling bell at the door announced Bill and Paul who walked in with coffee from High Winds.

"Well, if it isn't Mr. Bill," Taylor teased. "Paul, I'm glad you dragged him from the Loon to join our coffee klatch."

"It didn't take much dragging this morning," Paul smiled.

"I'm not so unsociable," Bill said defensively. "I'm just selective in the company I keep."

"Well, in a small town, that means you are unsociable, right guys? I mean, look at who you're having coffee with," Taylor hooted a laugh. "Your hired gun, your high school football quarterback, and your tomboy girlfriend from sixth grade. I'd say that's a pretty select group, wouldn't you?"

"You weren't my girlfriend," Bill countered. "You were just the only girl who would talk back to me."

"Yeah, 'cause every other girl was afraid of you. Enough! You are welcomed at our table, and there's always room at a round table, and I've got a round table right here," she pointed to the table the group always sat at near the ice cream freezer case.

The guys sat down at a table, and Taylor asked, "Bill, pick your poison: Bayfield Bass cone, Bass Waffle, Cool Cream, or ice cream with or without berries? I already know that Chris and Paul will have their regular—Chris gets a Bass Waffle, Paul watches his slim figure and gets a Cool Cream—that's a flavored whipped cream, Bill, since I don't think you've ever been in here—Today's flavor is strawberry, and I usually have a bowl of berries. We carry Kigan's ice cream."

Bill didn't hesitate. "It's a bit early, but I have a weak spot for ice cream. And for Kigan's, I am a sucker. Do you have cherry?"

"Cherry it is!" Taylor exclaimed. Coming right up, and she went to the back to prepare the treats.

Bill got up from the table, coffee cup in hand and followed her behind the counter. "I didn't realize you had these specialty items. I'm curious about these waffles. I know your gramma used to make us flavored whipped cream. Is that what you're selling?"

I was selling Gramma Emmy's ice cream, but Kigan's is so good, and they make larger quantities, so I dropped making my own ice cream and just sell Chris's. So, I focus on the whipped creams and butter. Then I offer berries from the farm. I'm sure when the apples come in, I'll be selling those, too.

"The waffles have been a big hit. Some days I haven't been able to keep up; the Bayfield Bass Cones I can make ahead of time, but the Bass Waffles are made to order. Here, I'll show you." And she proceeded to pour batter into two halves of a fish shaped griddle, then put a dab of chocolate in the middle. She did this to four griddles. Then folded the griddles together. "I'm making you a treat, Mr. Bill." She smiled at him and winked.

She scooped a dish of cherry ice cream from the bucket in the display freezer, put a spoon in it and handed it to Bill. "Go on out to the table, I'll bring the rest." He did as directed, ice cream in one hand, coffee cup in the other.

Taylor followed him, the aroma of fresh baked waffles filling the air, a bowl of strawberries and a bowl of strawberry flavored whipped cream all on a serving tray. She handed out the treats, and then handed Bill a small paper tray with a golden-brown fish shaped waffle. "This is a Bass Waffle. It's originally a Japanese specialty called a *taiyaki*. We also make a fish cone filled with Cool Cream or ice cream. The fish cones are called Bayfield Bass, you may have heard people talking about them. I hope you like it," she said shyly.

"I made one for each of us, so don't think I'm treating Bill special or anything," she said, admonishing Chris and Paul before they could protest.

Chris, Paul and Taylor paused to watch Bill take his first bite of the Bass Waffle. They watched as he blew on it to cool it, then sunk his teeth into the head of the fish. A little bit of chocolate oozed from the wound. He chewed and swallowed, then immediately took his next bite. Smiles began lighting up the faces of his audience. This bite they knew had more chocolate in it.

"Oh my god, these fish are to die for. Where did these come from? We should franchise them!" Bill was over the top enthusiastic.

"Well, right now I just want to be able to pay back my loan and hire some help, but yeah, let's franchise and make millions—after I pay back the loan," Taylor said laughing. "I'm glad you like them. Let's make millions later. Right now, I just have to make it through the 4th of July." The four friends at the table all burst into laughter, and casual chatter continued. Customers began to slowly wander into the store, following the wafting aroma of the waffles.

The four stood up, coffee klatch over. "OK, Bill, just want you to know that if you show up for coffee tomorrow, you might be sitting here alone. Mondays are our Sundays, and it's my one day off. You are welcome to stop in, just saying…" Taylor said to Bill.

"Thanks for the heads up. I would have been here, for sure. I'm going out tomorrow. You want to sail with me and Paul?" he asked.

"Gosh, I haven't been out in ages. You know us locals don't get to go out on sailboats that often. We're more of the ferry and speedboat crowd, usually because we're in a hurry; we don't have time to lollygag about. Offers to sail don't come too often; I can't say 'no,' so I guess that's a qualified 'yes,' isn't it? I'd love to, thank you, Bill."

"Great. I like to get started early, so come by the Loon around 7 am. Not too early, is it?"

"You're talking to a small business owner whose days start at 5 am. I can sleep in and still be there on time. See you then," Taylor replied.

Bill smiled and walked out of the shop. Taylor thought she heard him whistling a tune—that tune by Bill Withers, *Lovely Day*--as he stepped out onto the street.

Chapter 11

Monday morning promised to be a perfect day for sailing. Winds out of the southeast, 10-15 knots, sunny, blue skies. The streets were still empty, weekenders either gone or sleeping in, shopkeepers slow to get going after the weekend rush. Taylor drove down the hill from the orchard and ambled down Rittenhouse Avenue. She pulled over in front of the shop, but didn't go in. She just looked quickly in the window, made a visual sweep of the front of the building, made a couple mental notes on some paint touch up needed above the door, and pulled back out and headed to the marina.

There was more activity at the marina. Early morning boaters were making their way to the showers in the marina office building, and a couple were headed to the Bayfield Yacht Club with a bag of groceries, likely planning to make themselves some breakfast. Taylor pulled her truck into a parking slot and grabbed her day bag that had a jacket, swimsuit, two peanut butter and raspberry jelly sandwiches, celery and carrot sticks to snack on. She had thrown in two White Claw seltzers and a bottle of wine. She put on her Cool Creams and Berries baseball cap and checked that she had thrown a couple extra caps into her bag.

She knew the Loon. It was the one sailing boat that was front and center in the marina if you were looking from the shore. She walked down the dock; her striped T, Capri pants and deck shoes made her look like a seasoned sailor. Bill was coming up from the cabin when he caught sight of her. He waved and said, "Ahoy! You look ready for the day! Bright and early, I like a woman who arrives on time. Come on down, throw your gear in the front cabin."

"Do you have a fridge or a cooler down there?" Taylor asked as she stepped from the dock to the boat deck, and then swung her leg over the ledge and onto the seat of the cockpit. She moved with the easy confidence of a woman who had been on a boat a time or two. "I have a little something for you," Taylor said as she reached into her bag. She pulled out a cap that matched her own. This one's for you. I have one for Paul, too."

"Paul wanted the day off today. He said Chris asked him to spend the day with his family on the dairy farm. Paul said he was interested in the farm, and wanted to get to know Chris's family, so I'm going to have to enlist you to help, if you don't mind, Taylor. It was kind of a last-minute deal," Bill said.

"No worries, matey. I'd love to help. I'd rather help. I don't like just sitting around, and this is a fabulous opportunity to learn something new. Put me in, coach!"

"OK, well, let's get going. There's a fridge on the starboard side as you go down into the cabin, and then would you get the checklist that's on the map table? That way we won't forget anything major," Bill said, turning to retrieve the boat hook from the storage under the bench and checking the halyard lines.

Taylor threw down her bag in the fore cabin, put the White Claws into the refrigerator, and set the sandwiches in the sink so they wouldn't shift around. She took a quick look around at the warm teakwood shelves and cupboards, the folded tables, the cushioned settees. Bill called down, "Hey Taylor, before you come up, would you grab the autopilot to the right of the map table? It's got buttons on the front…"

Taylor scanned the table and the area to the right. She saw what Bill described, and called back up, "Aye, aye, sir. Anything else?"

"Look at the checklist. I know you have to flip the electronics switch and the VHF 16 switch, can you do that—on the switch board?" Taylor saw what he was talking about and flipped the switches to "on".

"All done, Bill. I'm coming up." And she clambered up the steps through the hatch, autopilot box in hand.

Bill and Taylor went through the checklist together, Bill explaining the items Taylor wasn't familiar with. She had done a considerable amount of boating, just not a lot of work on a sailboat. They used the diesel engine to motor out of the marina, and when they cleared the entrance and moved beyond the Madeline Island ferry route, Bill turned the boat into the wind and called Taylor to the helm and told her to keep the boat facing into the wind. He then began to hoist the mainsail and unfurl the headsail.

They turned north, Bill cut the engine and the sails filled with the breeze. They were on their way.

The day flew by. Bill and Taylor began to reacquaint each to the other as adults and old friends who had been out of touch for years. They fell into a comfortable rhythm that they hadn't had since the sixth grade. It was warm, a high close to 90, and the water temperature at the surface close to 70. That was extremely warm for this early in the season. They sailed to Stockton Island, and dropped anchor in Julian Bay which was more protected from the wind that had shifted to coming out of the south.

Bill lowered the Zodiac dinghy into the clear waters of Superior and Taylor climbed over the stern and down the ladder into the rubber dinghy that took them to shore. As she turned back, the low sleek profile and teak trimmed beauty of the Loon caught her breath.

They pulled the dinghy onto shore and began a short hike to the ranger station on the far side of Presque Isle Point. As they wandered around inside the visitor center, front and center was a stuffed black bear, Scar, that had tipped one too many garbage cans near campers. It was the demise of the bear, but a skilled taxidermist kept the spirit of Scar on the island. Bill and Taylor wandered through the exhibits until they reached the disk where the ranger, a woman whose enthusiasm for the island was unparalleled, stood speaking to a small group of tourists. She raved about the Indian Pipe plants that had just begun to bloom and the Butter and Eggs wild snapdragons that could be found along the campsite trail. They learned about the singing sands on Julian Bay, which were, according to the ranger, a 'must hear' attraction.

Bill and Taylor hiked the Anderson Point Trail back to Julian Bay, and as they rounded the last bend of the trail over the red flat rocks along the water, a view of the Loon greeted them, patiently waiting. As they walked the beach of Julian Bay, they delighted in hearing the 'singing sands', just as the ranger had predicted.

It was early afternoon by the time they made it back to the Loon, tired but happy. While Bill had shared past experiences with Taylor, they also had the joy and excitement of having the discovered the 'singing sands' together.

They secured the dinghy to the rear of the Loon and pulled anchor. "Oh, Bill. You know how lucky you are to have a boat as lovely as the Loon?" Taylor asked him.

He shrugged. "It's normal to me now. I know that sounds extraordinarily entitled, but a person gets used to it all after a while. It makes me wonder what's really important, and the Loon only complicates matters."

"Well, I think the Loon is amazing, and even if *you* don't feel lucky, *I* feel lucky to have had this day with her. Thank you."

"It's been a good day for me, too. You're easy to be with, Taylor. And you seem so comfortable on the Loon. It's fun to watch you learning how she works. You know we need to name the dinghy. What do you think might fit?" he asked her, changing the subject to a lighter one.

"Well, if the dinghy is a baby of the Loon, and she rides on her back, what are baby loons called?" Taylor asked. Her thinking out loud was fun to follow.

"I think baby loons are chicks, but I'd have to Google it to be sure. The dinghy can be called 'The Chick', you think?" he asked her.

Taylor laughed out loud. "That would be fun. And so appropriate. How clever we are!"

"We make a good team, you're a great first mate, Taylor!"

"That we are," Taylor replied. "I'd like to talk to you more about franchising. Were you serious when you talked about it at the shop?"

"Well, yes, I was," Bill said. "I was totally impressed with the concept. It's a bit out of my business realm, so what I would recommend is to put a marketing team on the project and do some due diligence to test how viable the business model might be."

"I know how that would work at Target, we had a whole team of people who did new business analysis. But I'm out of my depth outside of corporate America. And I don't have the funds to finance it myself yet. I'm just launching Cool Creams." Taylor had a furrowed brow as she was thinking it through.

"I could bring it before my board to see if they'd be interested in financing a viability assessment. There'd be a significant amount of research to go into it, and if we decide not to pursue it, you'd be set up to offer it to other investors. "We would have first right of refusal," Bill added. "You should think about it, for sure."

"Of course I will," Taylor said. "I'd be crazy not to. And I would assume all of this would take some time, anyway. I appreciate your offer to help, and I wouldn't even probably consider this if it were anyone but you."

Bill agreed, "I know you've had some solid corporate experience, otherwise I wouldn't be talking about this with you. You've got the marketing touch—it's obvious with what you are doing at Cool Creams. But franchising is another kind of fish, and in my experience, it takes a different kind of strategy. But it would be fun to work with you on a project like this. I'll call the office and have them write up an agreement to do preliminary due diligence to see if it's viable for my venture capital company. We would need your financials and if you have a business plan, we'd need that. It would be interesting to see if our teamwork skills would generalize from the boat to business."

Taylor smiled at him warmly, comfortable in the way they talked to each other, as friends and equals. "Assuming the agreement keeps everything confidential, I'd be happy to share my books with your group, and I had to write a business plan for the bank to get the operating capital.

This could be loads of fun," Taylor said.

They sailed back to the marina, taking a few tacks on their way into the wind. As they dropped sail and motored into the marina, the sun was setting over the hills behind Bayfield. Taylor put on her jacket—the breeze off the cool waters of Lake Superior made an evening chill—and Paul greeted them at their slip and helped them dock. Taylor threw the dock lines out to Paul, and he quickly secured them to the cleats. She had put the fenders out earlier, and the Loon bumped gently against them.

Paul offered to secure the boat, which freed Bill and Taylor to walk together to the Bistro to grab dinner. The peanut butter sandwiches had been devoured hours ago and they were both famished. Monday nights were slow at the Manypenny Bistro, and they walked into the bar and sat at a high top.

Neither wanted the evening to end. Taylor had a White Claw, Bill had an Old Milwaukee in the spirit of Wisconsin, and they settled back after ordering their burger and a 10-inch pesto pizza. Taylor's nose was tinged red from too much sun, a faint spattering of freckles dotted across her cheekbones. She had put on her jacket to ward off the chill that often comes from getting too much sun during the day. Bill, more acclimated to being exposed to the sun and wind after weeks of sailing, looked tanned and relaxed. Clearly sailing was his happy place.

Taylor began. "Tell me how it was for you after we graduated. The two of us were always head-to-head. Was it hard at Stanford? Was California all surfing and blonde girls? Like here?" She laughed in self-deprecation. She realized how silly that sounded. Back when they had grown up and gone to school, except for a handful of Native and Hispanic kids, it was an almost all-white community where most of their classmates looked like Chris Kigan. She knew now that school demographics had changed.

"It wasn't so bad. I always say the hardest part of going to Stanford was getting in. Once they have you, they want you to succeed. They work hard to make sure the students have the support they need to make it," Bill explained. "Stanford's in Northern California, so there's not much surfing. It's too cold during the school year. And the girls weren't all blonde. Actually, the student body is pretty diverse. It was like being dumped in the proverbial melting pot. There are kids from all over the US and the world. In all shapes and sizes and colors. I loved it there," he said with a faraway look. "I think I fell in love several times, but nothing ever lasted. It was great fun," he added.

"I was so envious when you left," Taylor said. "After the announcement of the class ranking, I got a lot of kudos, but the spotlight was on you, you know. But I had a great time at Madison. You know it's the party school, and it lived up to the reputation. At first everyone was pushing the limit but by the end of sophomore year, or maybe even freshman year, the partying got old, and most of us got down to business."

"Well, I wouldn't describe Stanford as a party school," Bill laughed. "The students come all so serious, ready to crack the next computer code, and it takes work to get them to lighten up. I'm not sure I ever lightened up…"

"We can change that, can't we?" Taylor challenged. "It's entirely up to us. 'I am the master of my fate, I am the captain of my soul,' remember that from English lit class? I think of it every day. I think it's true. We all don't have the same opportunities, but what's vital? Family. Friends. The Orchard. Our community, wherever that is. You've done so much with your life already. So, we got a couple of curve balls thrown at us. So what. We have at least three more quarters to play."

"Aside from mixing metaphors and confusing your sports, I think you are spot on, Taylor."

Their food arrived, and their conversation waned as they ate. Bill raved about the pesto pizza, as a 'hidden diamond.' As the server took their plates, Bill pushed back from the table, with a low moan. "That was great. I'm beat. How about you?"

"I'm beat, too. What a great day, thanks so much. I didn't know what to expect, spending a day with you. It was special, Bill, I am pleasantly happy," Taylor smiled, her eyes closed, her head back, exposing her neck to Bill.

"I'll walk you back to your truck. You work tomorrow, right?"

"Aww, yeah, I work tomorrow. As Scarlett O'Hara famously said, 'I'll think about that tomorrow. Tomorrow is another day.'"

"And I can attest, 'As God is [your] witness, [you'll] never go hungry again!' or at least for tonight. Alright, my Scarlett, time to go home," Bill said as he grabbed Taylor by the hand and pulled her from the stool.

They left the Bistro and walked arm in arm back to the marina parking lot. They got to Taylor's truck, and Taylor leaned into him. She turned and looked up to Bill, clearly ready and willing.

Bill gave her a long hug, responding to her offer. Then he pulled away. "You work tomorrow. I can drive you home if you want, but home is where you're headed, my dear."

Taylor straightened up, pulled her jacket close around her, and said with great composure, "I can drive myself. Thanks for a nice day." A chill settled on them both as she got into her truck and didn't look back as she drove away. She didn't see Bill standing in the lot watching her leave. He stood in the lot long after he couldn't see her any longer, gazing at the empty street, a small frown on his brow.

Chapter 12

Bill lay in his aft berth, thinking about the course of the day, how as the hours passed Taylor became more and more lovely. Her sunny disposition, her frank and curious demeanor, her willingness to try and do anything was refreshing and attractive. And there was comfort in having a long history with her. He knew her as a child, and now as a woman. And while the outer trappings changed, the inner core of steely determination was still what made her who she was. She was attractive, but his real life was in Chicago. She was part of a temporary reprieve—a summer vacation from real life.

That's what held him back. He knew that if she didn't mean anything to him, it would have been easy to be lying together, in this berth this very instant. But it wasn't so easy to undo things with a valuable friend. And he didn't think of her as a convenience. She was a good friend—a best friend—from childhood. They had fought on the playground and fought in the classroom for recognition and for top grades. She was likely the reason he had gotten into Stanford—their fight for the top grades constantly pushed him to do better. Their bond went deep as both friends and competitors. That was too much to jeopardize. He turned to his side, closed his eyes but couldn't sleep. He saw her on the deck of the Loon securing lines. He saw her at the helm as he attended to the sails. He saw her hiking in front of him, hair swaying in rhythm to her steps. It was as if he was seeing her in his mind's eye walking in front of him leading the way, and with the Loon gently rocking, he finally fell asleep.

Taylor was having trouble falling asleep, too, but for different reasons. *Why didn't he want me to stay?* She asked herself. The signals seemed to be there. Things were clicking. She didn't want to go home. She wanted to continue to feel the rocking of the Loon. And things felt so…*simpatico*. The word popped into her head. She felt as though she could have talked to him all day and all night.

And he was still so sexy. She had to admit to herself that it wasn't just his intellect that was attractive. His whole being sucked her in. She pictured him standing on the flat red rocks of Anderson Trail, looking towards the Loon. She placed a hand on her chest as she felt herself being pulled towards him. *Oh my,* she thought. *I have it bad.*

She tossed and turned, images of the day floating above her, until the light, grey streaks of early dawn began to brush the eastern sky. Then she fell into a restless sleep.

Chapter 13

He woke early and called his office in Chicago to get them working on an agreement for Taylor. Then he walked up the hill to the Boyt homeplace to check on the repair progress. The shingles had finally arrived in Duluth, and Rick was going to be driving to pick them up. Painting crews were setting up for some of the detail work on the gingerbread trim. He could see the light at the end of the repair tunnel. He wasn't needed there, so he walked to the Madeline Island Ferry boat landing where the ferries docked.

Ambitious tourists were lining up to spend the day on Madeline Island, and a few more were checking out the tour boat options. Families in clusters were forming as one parent or the other went to buy the tickets. The happy sounds of vacationers played as background music to his thoughts. *This is nice,* he thought. *People are happy here. They're on vacation. They are spending the time hiking, biking, camping, sailing, boating, kayaking, burning off the adrenalin that builds up in the city. They're rested, relaxed, anticipating the day or the week. Yes, this is nice.*

He walked towards the Bayfield Marina where the Loon was docked, taking the walking path closest to the water. *It was going to be another lovely day in paradise,* he thought. He reboarded the Loon and thought of the next project he was going to be working on. The list was endless.

Little did he know of the excitement happening on Rittenhouse Avenue at this very moment. Chris and Paul had gotten their coffees and were just beginning to tell Taylor about their day on the farm when the bell announced a visitor. A tall, sleek brunette walked in. They stopped talking.

Barbie, was the first thing Taylor thought when she saw the woman. Too tall, too skinny, too perfect. Her nails were a bright red. She had clearly gone shopping at an upscale store if the brand-new Sperry Top Siders, white cotton sailing sweater, and bright-white shorts were any indication. She was carrying a Dooney and Bourke hobo bag with enough intentional casualness that it screamed expensive. A cute red Porsche Boxster was parked out on the street. Taylor wondered if the two went together. Her nails were the same color as the car. They got all kinds of tourists at Bayfield, but the Apostles were a national lakeshore; most of the people were sporty casual--Patagonia fleece and REI backpackers--not Marina del Rey look-at-me types.

Chris and Paul gave the woman a once over, and then looked at each other. Some unspoken understanding passed between them. Taylor stood up from the round table the three of them were sharing, and said, "Hi, welcome to Cool Creams. I'm the owner, can I help you?" She wondered, *who is this woman? She's definitely not the waffles and ice cream type. Based on her looks, she's a Keto Diet, bottled water type.*

"I'm actually looking to meet up with my husband? I wasn't sure where to find him? I would guess at a marina? He sailed here about a month ago? His name is Bill Boyt." Every sentence ended in a question mark, except the last.

It was like in the movies when there's a shift in a tectonic plate. The world seemed to tilt for everyone in the room, for different reasons.

Taylor's mouth hung open for a few seconds too long, and Paul came to her rescue. "Ah, Mrs. Boyt," Paul oozed. "You are very close. Mr. Boyt is at the marina, just down the street. I am his sailing mate, Paul. It would be my pleasure to take you down to the Loon."

Just then the bells tinkled again, and in walked Sue Boyt, wearing cargo shorts, a chamber of commerce polo shirt and arms full of 4th of July brochures. She stopped short and looked at the back of the tall woman. Chris, Paul, and Taylor were still gaping, too. "Brenda?" Sue said quite incredulously. "Brenda, is that you?"

Brenda—now that they knew her name—turned and looked over Sue's head, then readjusted her regal pose and looked down her nose to meet Sue's eyes. "Ah. Sue. My dear," she said in a stilted manner. And she bent stiffly at the waist and gave Sue a cursory hug.

Then Sue did something really funny, but at which no one dared laugh. She said, in a stilted manner matching Brenda's from a moment ago, "Ah. Brenda. My dear," Sue echoed.

Taylor stood up straighter and held out her hand. "I'm Taylor. I went to school with Bill. This is Chris Kigan, he went to school with Bill, too. I'm sure we will have a chance later to get to know each other better, but if you want to catch Bill, you might want to get down to the marina. I heard he might be heading out on the Loon this morning." That wasn't true, but she was anxious to get this woman out of her shop.

Brenda turned to Paul and said, "Would you be so kind…" and Paul led her out of the shop, glancing over his shoulder at the three of them as he walked out after Brenda. Taylor, Sue, and Chris gawked as the two paused by the red Porsche. They could see them paused by the front of the car to talk but couldn't hear the words. Brenda got into the convertible, turned the key. It roared to life. Then, they began a strange parade, she drove behind Paul as he walked down Rittenhouse to South 1st Street. She slowly turned right onto 1st, still following Paul who kept walking.

Taylor turned to Sue. "Sue, call Bill right now. You better warn him what's headed his way. We'd hate to see him capsize in the middle of the marina."

Sue pulled her phone out, dialed and was waiting for Bill to pick up. "Bill," she said into the receiver. "A storm's blown in. It's headed your way right now. Batten down the hatches, Brenda's in town."

Sue shoved her cell phone into her back pocket. Taylor looked around and realized the three of them were still standing in the front of the shop, still staring out the front window towards the Porsche that was long gone.

Chris broke the silence that hung in the air. "Wow."

That was all it took and the three of them burst into laughter. Sue plopped down in the chair Paul had vacated, Taylor went behind the counter and poured batter in the griddle to make three Bass Waffles. "Pick your poison: chocolate, strawberry, or caramel?"

Chris said, "I'll try the caramel. Is that something new?"

Sue said, "Chocolate with a dab of strawberry please."

Taylor brought the finished waffles out and sat down between the two. "Yeah, I saw those old caramel squares at the grocery store and thought I'd try them. It's pretty good."

"OK, Sue, it's time to spill your guts. Give us the lowdown on Brenda. Now I understand why none of us have ever met her. She's… amazing." Taylor finished on an openly positive note, but she had a questioning look on her face and she had had to search for a word to describe Brenda. Chris sat quietly, watching the two women. Sue had picked up Paul's coffee and was drinking it absent-mindedly.

Sue started chuckling. "Well, I never met her until the week of the wedding. It was a big shindig in Chicago. Yeah, picture me at a big society wedding in the city. I was the proverbial fish out of water. But I grit my teeth and tolerated it for Bill. I was the only person from Bayfield. Bill had his group of buddies from Stanford stand up with him—nice group of guys—but it was all Brenda and Brenda's friends, or entourage. Best thing about the wedding was the all-you-could-drink bar. I don't remember much else, compliments of the open bar. I didn't stay long. I recall Brenda's dad being a nice man. Her mom is just like her, just an older version."

"I can understand," Chris interjected. "She's beautiful. She's like an exotic animal. I mean, really, we all couldn't stop looking at her. She oozes confidence that makes her like ice, yes, but she is, ah, I mean, most guys I know would only dream of getting her… I mean, I can see how Bill got ensnarled in that woman's web…She's like a Lauren Bacall with dark hair…"

Taylor and Sue just sat absorbing what Chris had said. Taylor was imagining Bill ensnarled in a web. Sue was thinking of the icy coolness she had always felt when she was around Brenda. Chris was thinking how lucky he was that she didn't interest him in the least.

Sue was always puzzled about how Bill had ended up with the likes of Brenda, but Chris was right. Brenda was striking and could draw a crowd around her like no one she had ever known. Bill just got stuck in the goo.

Chapter 14

Bill was on the deck of the Loon when he got the call. He had been considering sailing out to the islands to take advantage of the breeze coming off the hills to the west, but his heart fell when he heard the news. At first, he considered heading out of the marina to avoid the confrontation coming at him. As he assessed that option, he knew he couldn't ready fast enough to take the Loon out before she got there. He looked out towards Madeline Island, tracking the ferry on its way to La Pointe. He had a moment when he wished he were on that ferry, escaping the conflict that was headed his way.

He saw Paul walking towards the marina parking lot, the fiery red Porsche slowly following him. He thought how hard that must be for the sports car, the gear ratios not made for going slow. *She's probably riding the clutch,* he was thinking. *What's she doing here? She hates sailing.* But as he watched Paul leading her down the dock to the Loon and to him, his heart clutched in his chest. *She's so beautiful,* he thought. *She broke my heart,* he reminded himself.

In an instant he remembered how it felt to walk into a room with Brenda on his arm. Heads would turn to look at her--at them--the glittering couple of the season. It was fun, in its own way. And there were times she was fun to be with, debriefing a party after the fact, her scathing remarks ripping at other women, and some of the men. He would laugh along with her, a persistent discomfort underlying it all. But she was all his—this perfectly put together, dark-haired beauty was all his, or so he thought.

"Bill, so here you are. I've missed you, darling. I'm so sorry to have been gone for so long myself." Of course, no reference to her backgammon side dish. She turned to Paul, "Would you get my bag out of the car? It's in the frunk. Front trunk."

"Bill, lend me your hand to help me in. You know I'm not a fan of these rocking boats. "You're looking particularly handsome this morning," she observed him carefully, noting the worn jeans hanging just so off his hips, the mid-weight cotton striped sweater, barefoot with a Cool Creams baseball cap on. A shortly cropped beard made him look like a younger version of the Dos Equis beer commercial's 'most interesting man in the world.'

"Paul, don't bother getting Brenda's bag," Bill ordered, while still reaching out to steady Brenda. "Call the Bayfield Inn and get her a room. Brenda, you're prone to seasickness, and we don't have room on the Loon anyway.

"I was just readying to go out. You can stay or go."

Paul was standing on the dock, uncertain what to do next. Then Bill said, "Paul, would you release the dock lines and come aboard? Brenda, if you are going to stay, you better sit down before you fall down." Brenda plopped down, her floppy sun hat askew. Bill was all business. He revved the diesel, pulled the Loon out of its slip, and headed to open water.

What a difference 24 hours makes. Yesterday he was relaxed and happy, focused on the horizon with Taylor on board. Today he kept looking at

Brenda nervously, wondering when this walking time bomb was going to explode. Brenda never just "dropped in." She had an agenda, and it was just a matter of time for her to bring it up. He was glad Paul was with them, a moderating factor hovering in the background.

They were heading northwest through the West Channel, the course set. Bill handed the helm to Paul and went below deck. Brenda followed. Bill stood at the kitchen refrigerator, rummaging for breakfast. He pulled out an orange juice and a Danish. As he stood facing the stove and sink, Brenda sidled up to him and put her arms around his waist, laid her cheek against his back. She could feel him stiffen.

"Oh, Bill, I've missed you. I'm sorry you left, I've missed you in my bed, at the dinner table, at parties. We are the best, you know. No one can work a crowd like you and I can. I've realized so much since you've been gone. So much I've taken for granted. I'll never take you for granted again, I promise," she cooed, her leg curling around his thigh.

He tilted his head back, felt her breath on his ear, making his scalp tingle. She could always do this to him. She had a power he didn't understand. He turned into her, and she pressed into him, pushing him back into the counter. Bill closed his eyes, letting himself fall backwards in time, to when they had first met, to that glorious feeling of abandon, trusting his emotional self to this woman. She was the woman who knew him best, had held him on those nights when business deals were hanging by a thread, not knowing if they'd be celebrating the next day or wondering how to handle investors. *If I could snap my fingers and go back to before, I would,* he thought.

He let her seduce him. He couldn't help it. His response was automatic. Her hands on his back moved to his hips. He pushed into her, feeling her offer herself up. He had loved this woman like no other, had waited to marry until he was sure, could still hear the words, "to love and to cherish from this day forward." He continued to keep his eyes closed, it was better that way. He could block out reality, just let himself fall into the fantasy.

She continued working her charm when a wake hit from a passing boat that set the Loon rocking. Bill's eyes popped open; he looked left and up just to catch Paul staring down at them. He looked over the top of Brenda's head to the map table where a woman's pair of Ray Bans caught his eye. Taylor's.

Then the other memories flooded back, to the moment he opened their bedroom door to see her with another man, her long bare leg exposed from the rumpled sheet, the man's arms wrapped around her, a look of shocked recognition on all their faces. The disbelief of seeing a man he had known for years and played backgammon with; gripping a clump of his wife's hair. The wretched feeling of betrayal overwhelmed him.

He pushed Brenda away and turned towards the sink. "No, Brenda. What's going on. Why now? What happened? What was so time sensitive that you followed me here. I don't need you; I don't want you. You shouldn't be here."

She tried to pull him back in, but he resisted, more forcefully this time. She backed away, sensing the heat of her body aligned with his wasn't enough. The magnetic force was broken. He was going to require more. She smoothed down her sweater and stood up straighter. "Daddy was sick. He was in the hospital for a while. He really needed you. **We** really need you, Bill," she said quietly. He thought she might begin crying. She had always been a daddy's girl.

"I'm sorry to hear that, but what can I do? I'm not part of his business, his investments are sound, I can't imagine what he would need from me," Bill said, a comforting hand on Brenda's shoulder. "But of course I will do whatever I can. I respect your dad. He's always been the best to me." Brenda peeked out from her hair to Bill's face. She realized this tact might work better.

"He needs your help, Bill. We don't have anyone to advise us. Would you come back with me, to help set up some of his estate plans? I need… I need…" she mewed like a kitten.

But then another swell came through the cabin, and Brenda felt her face go green. "I'm going to be sick! Move out of the way!" and she headed to the aft head. Bill heard her retching but didn't go to her right away. It reminded him why she never sailed. In addition to the fact hauling on rope lines to raise the mainsail or unfurl the jib, wrapping lines around a winch or working a winch handle could jeopardize her immaculately manicured nails or blister her soft and pampered palms. And putting on makeup in the tiny head was virtually impossible. He realized these facts about Brenda never bothered him before until he found in Taylor that all women weren't fixated on their outer shell.

He followed her aft and saw her bent over, her hair hiding her face. She continued to heave. He sat on the bed, contemplating her hind end hanging out of the head. She was still beautiful, even in distress. "Brenda, sometimes it helps to lie down. You can use my bed here," he offered.

She backed out and made a quarter turn to the bed. It was tight quarters in the sloop--efficient, but tight. He helped her under the covers, gave her a plastic bag, and said, "I'm going topside." And he began to go forward.

He called out to her, "We'll head back to the marina and drop you off. No sense in trying to make this work," and he went on deck for the rest of the journey.

He took back the helm from Paul, who busied himself preparing to dock. As Bill gazed out across the water, scanning the mainland starboard and Basswood Island portside, he realized what he was really looking forward to was going to Cool Creams and Berries and spending time with Taylor.

Chapter 15

It was later that morning when Kent came in the back door of Cool Creams and Berries with the summer's first flat of raspberries in hand. "Hello!" he called out. Sue met him in the back room. She greeted him by putting her cheek against his, chaste yet intimate.

"Hi," she said shyly. "I wondered when you'd be coming in. I have some news for you.

"Taylor ran to the bank; she'll be right back. I'm helping her prep for the 4th," she said. She was still a bit unfamiliar with the change in their relationship. They had been living and working in the Bayfield community for years, yet it was unclear what was different in this particular season that made them recognize and acknowledge the spark between them. Maybe it was seeing the aging process in action that made them realize how time marches on.

"I'll just put these berries into the cooler, and come up front," Kent said. "What was it you wanted to tell me?"

Sue put a Bass Waffle in front of Kent as he sat down. He looked comfortable in his worn cotton plaid shirt and bib overalls. It surprised her how endearing the smile wrinkles around his eyes made him look to her. She put her hand on his arm. "Bill's ex showed up this morning. She didn't just show up, she roared in here and roared out. I think our heads are still spinning. Chris and Paul were here, too. Paul took her down to the docks, or I should say he led her down to the docks... I'm not sure what Taylor's feeling. She buried herself in the backroom, and just left a few minutes ago."

"Oh, well, that complicates things a bit, doesn't it?" Kent pondered. "How does Bill feel about her—what's her name again?"

"Brenda. And you know he didn't leave her, he caught her with a friend of his. He was blistered from that breach of confidence, I can tell you that. I'm sure he thought it was forever… He's that kind of guy. So I don't know what's going to happen. I know he wanted his marriage to work, but how badly, I don't know. And I'm not sure what brought that little hussy back to town.

"She definitely makes a statement, I can tell you that, for sure," Sue rambled on. "Her and this hot red convertible, and not just any convertible, but a high-end fancy one. And she looks like, I don't know, there's nothing like her around this town. She looks like a magazine model."

"Then I can't wait to meet her," Kent said jokingly. "But not really," he said in a conciliatory tone. "I couldn't afford her, I'm sure."

"You got that right, Buddy," Sue countered. The front door opened, and Chris came in just as Taylor, who had parked in the alley, walked in from the back.

"Who's throwing the party?" Taylor asked.

"No party, I'm just curious. I don't want to miss any of the action," Chris replied from the front of the shop. "Any news updates?" Everyone knew what he was referring to.

Then Paul came in the front door, completing the quintet. All eyes were on him. He looked cool in his cotton sweater, cargo shorts and boat shoes. His dark skin glowed—he obviously had walked from the Loon. "You didn't have to have a party for me, you know," he bantered. "I should have printed a news bulletin, since I know that's what you're all waiting for.

"Oh, hi, Kent," Paul nodded to Kent. He pulled up a chair.

"She's quite a number," Paul began. Taylor had stayed behind the counter, not sure she wanted to fully engage. She definitely had mixed feelings about the morning. And wanted to know more, but also didn't want to intrude on Bill's personal life, nor did she want to admit that all those old sweetheart feelings for him had resurfaced from their day sailing.

"And she has a lot of baggage." There were a few eyebrows that rose on that statement. Paul realized what that sounded like, and said, "No, I mean literally. She has a lot of baggage with her, every compartment and passenger seat were full of suitcases and duffels. That's why I had to walk down to the dock. There was no place for me to sit."

There was a general nodding of understanding among the group. They had all wondered why he had walked, and she had driven behind. "We thought that was kinda weird," Sue said for the group. "So, then what?"

"We went sailing. She doesn't know much about sailing, so Bill and I got underway, then I took the helm, and Bill went below deck. She followed him, and they were down there for a while. I couldn't see them for the most part, I mean, they were all over each other near the kitchen (sorry,

Taylor), and then she went aft, and a bit later Bill came up alone and we turned and came back.

He got her a room at the Bayfield Inn. I take it she gets seasick, so she doesn't stay onboard," Paul finished. "That's why I know she has baggage. I carried it all to her room at the Inn."

Taylor had listened stock still, absorbing each word, picturing in her mind the scenario. Bill, tall and slender, moving below deck. Brenda, also tall and slender, following behind him. The two of them close together. And then going aft, where she knew Bill's cabin was. Where she knew his bed was. She forced herself to focus on the group in front of her. She didn't want to imagine what happened in his cabin, but she couldn't help but see in her mind's eye the two of them entwined in make-up sex. That's what happens in real life. Men just can't resist the draw of an available, willing woman. Except that Bill had done exactly that last night when she was ready, but he was unwilling. She was beginning to get angry—anger camouflaged the hurt that stung her heart.

Chris interjected himself into her reveries. "OK, I know we can all imagine what was going on, but we don't know, and she did just show up unannounced. We would have known if Bill had asked her to come up. I think we can assume she just showed up."

Sue followed that line of thinking, "I'm pretty sure Bill would never have asked her to come. Their divorce is finalized, or darned near final I'm pretty sure. I mean, this was part of his healing journey, right? I mean…" And then the bells announced a customer, or more precisely, announced Bill.

He stepped into the doorway and stopped short. He surveyed the table where Kent, Sue, Chris and Paul all sat. His eyes met Taylor's; she was still behind the counter. "Oh. Hi, everyone. I didn't realize you were all here," he said tentatively, still looking at Taylor.

"Come on in, we were just talking about the 4th plans," Sue segued seamlessly. "We could use your input."

"Would you like anything?" Taylor asked him.

"You know, a Bayfield Bass cone with cherry ice cream would really hit the spot," he replied.

"Coming right up, sir," she replied. "Keep talking, guys, I can hear you while I prep."

"I'd like to invite you all to the Loon to watch fireworks on the 4th," Bill announced. If you'd bring hors d'oeuvres, I'll supply the drinks."

Kent laughed. "If you mean we bring snacks, that we can do."

"Best seats in the house," Sue added. "You can count us in," Kent nodded. Bill's eyebrows raised, realizing his sister was speaking for both Kent and herself.

"I'm in, thanks, Bill," Chris replied. "Appreciate it."

"Paul, of course you can join or do your own thing, you aren't on the clock. But you're more than welcomed," Bill said, not wanting Paul to feel obligated.

"There's not another group of people I'd rather be with, thanks," Paul responded to Bill but was looking at Chris.

Taylor came out from behind the counter with the Bayfield Bass in hand. She placed it in front of Bill and said, "The fourth is going to be really busy—I hope—I can't really commit 'til I know how the day takes shape. And I have that high school kid that will be helping… Thanks, but I'll have to get back to you. No rest for the wicked."

"I'd really like for you to come," Bill began when Sue asked bluntly, "Where's Brenda?" Taylor was relieved to have the attention taken off of her and directed to the elephant in the room.

"We deposited her at the Bayfield Inn. Paul did the heavy lifting, packing all her bags in for her. I imagine you all won't see her until the community pig roast on the 4th, if then. She got a little seasick on the boat."

"I'm taking her to dinner at the Copper Trout tonight, too," Bill added.

"Oh, yeah?" Sue prodded.

They all waited for him to expand on the topic, but he didn't take the bait. The gears in everyone's head were turning. The Copper Trout was the fanciest restaurant in town. Elegant white tablecloths, candles on the tables, mood lighting. It was definitely where a person took a special someone. And someplace where you went with someone, not solo. Taylor had never been there.

I may never go there, now, she thought to herself.

The bell on the door began ringing, and customers began trickling in. Taylor wiped her hands on her apron, and began to work, greeting customers and prepping the waffles. Sue got up to help her. Another workday was off and running.

Chapter 16

Sue was large and in charge over the course of the 4th of July celebration, culminating with the pig roast and fireworks. As part of her official duties as town mayor, she started the sailing regatta that was held right in front of the town between the marina and Madeline Island. Self-guided tours of the butterfly gardens included her own yard. The vendors' pop up canopies lined the streets. She introduced the Summer Scavenger Hunt that encouraged locals and tourists alike to explore the businesses in the area in search of "treasures" and trivia at each location. The activities and the inevitable crises that arose put Sue smack dab into her element.

She was sitting next to Jack, a high school classmate and Kent's best friend, at Morty's Pub having lunch when word reached her that the power for the vendors on Second Street had gone out. She scrolled through her contacts and reached Terry Mason, who worked for the power company and had been her date to the Junior/Senior prom. He solved the problem while she was finishing her chicken strips and cheese curds. Later, one of Chris Kigan's cousins, Jeannie the Nut Lady who sold roasted nuts, complained that the specialty popcorn vendor was stealing her customers. Sue placated the Nut Lady by buying nuts for the Chamber staff and moved the popcorn vendor around the corner.

Jack waited patiently, quiet as a mouse, knowing some of the people on the other end of the phone may have thought the town mayor worked from a lofty office at city hall. He wanted to keep up the image even though they were at Morty's, at the bar, having drinks stronger than Coca Cola for lunch.

"Can I help you with anything?" Jack asked. Sue looked at him sideways. Jack lacked organizational skills, and if anything, was only marginally reliable.

She thought, *No way, Jose.* But said, "Thanks, Jack, but things are under control. I appreciate the offer."

Every day was the same, just different problems to be solved, new issues to wrangle. Sue loved it all. Some days it was Jack sitting next to her; sometimes it was Kent. It didn't much matter most of the time, it was her kingdom, after all.

She helped out at Cool Creams and Berries when she could. Taylor had gotten a high school student to work during the week of the fourth, but the extra hands always helped. And it was centrally located so if she was called away, she could get anywhere within minutes.

She did wonder about her brother Bill. He seemed distracted. And with Brenda still in town, she worried about what was going on with that. She had good cause to worry, too.

Chapter 17

Brenda had only been in town for a few hours, but her impact was like a tsunami. The staff at the Bayfield Inn knew they had a special guest. It was the staff code for a demanding guest. As soon as she was checked in, she called room service.

"I'd like a salad, spring greens, make sure all the water is patted off. Balsamic vinegar on the side, no oil, with cherry tomatoes sliced in half, grated fresh parmesan cheese, and real bacon bits on the top. No cucumbers, no carrots. A glass of chardonnay from an unopened bottle, please. And a chocolate mint," she ordered from room service. She didn't question whether they had the ingredients she demanded. She assumed they did.

The seventeen-year-old senior in high school who took the order, just wrote everything down. She gave it to the cook, who took one look and said, "Fat chance." He reached into the cooler, passed the spring green bin and grabbed a handful of iceberg lettuce. He proceeded to sprinkle Kraft Parmesan cheese over it and laid two strips of bacon across the top. The girl who took the order was too young to pour wine, so the cook asked the bartender for a glass of white. The barkeep took the first bottle and filled the sturdy wine glass with a generous pour of Pinot Grigio. The cook put it all on a tray and in lieu of a chocolate mint, he placed a razor thin slice of flourless chocolate cake on a plate.

He handed it to the high school girl and told her, "Tell her we did the best we could with the ingredients we had and the cake is compliments of the chef," he said with a wink.

The terrified girl went up to Brenda's room with the tray. With a timid knock, she announced, "Room Service," and waited.

Brenda came to the door and ordered the girl to place the tray on her table. She lifted the cover over the salad and before she could say anything, the girl said, "We did the best we could with our ingredients. The cake is complimentary from the chef, ma'am."

"Well, I should have known," Brenda sighed. "Don't wait around for a tip, there's not one coming from me." And she pointed to the door.

Brenda sat at the table looking out over the marina. *It is a pretty little town,* she thought to herself. *But could Bill seriously consider staying here? I can't imagine. I've got to get him back to civilization and get him thinking straight. Straight to me.*

She took a sip of her wine. *Ewww, they can't even get a simple Chardonnay right.*

Chapter 18

While Brenda waited impatiently for Bill to arrive at the Copper Trout, there was another dinner party happening just down the street. Taylor flipped the Open sign to Closed and joined Kent and Sue at the round table next to the ice cream freezer. A few minutes later, Paul and Chris walked in carrying two pizzas from Sgt. Pepperoni's. Then the door opened again, and Jack walked in with two twelve packs of Bent Paddle, one pilsner and one adventure pack that had a variety of brews. He pulled up a chair from another table and squeezed himself between Kent and Sue.

Taylor got up, locked the door and announced, "The party can officially begin!"

Meanwhile, as Brenda tapped her foot on the hardwood floor, Bill sauntered in from the street, only ten minutes late. With a lightweight wool sweater draped over his shoulders and wearing khaki slacks, he looked the part of a sailor. He scanned the room and caught sight of Brenda as she was waving to catch his attention. Her impatience evaporated.

She stood tall and offered her cheek to him. He couldn't help admiring the long form, her shirt soft against his hands, tight jeans accentuating her thin waist and Barbie legs.

"Darling, I was so looking forward to dinner tonight. What have you been doing all day in this dreary little town? I can't believe you grew up here. Whatever did you do as a child? I'm sure the Fourth is the biggest thing in town..." she finally ran out of steam.

Bill avoided eye contact. Instead, he looked down. "I see you have a glass of wine. Have you had a chance to look at the menu?" he asked, then turned to the waiter. "I'll have a Bent Paddle pilsner, thanks."

He turned to Brenda. "They get their trout and whitefish fresh from the lake. You can't make a mistake ordering the fish here."

"Oh, fine, why don't you order for me, dear? You know better than I. I'm sure I'd end up with canned tuna," Brenda said, looking up at Bill through her lashes.

She looks exotic, Bill thought. *Too much makeup for Bayfield, but probably just right for a night out in Chicago.* He looked at her perfect skin, any imperfections covered with the makeup foundation expertly applied. He thought, *Porcelain. So that's where the term comes from. Her skin looks like porcelain. Almost translucent.*

She had a black silk shirt on, unbuttoned to the base of her sternum, tucked into jeans that left nothing to the imagination. The high heels with red soles shouted expensive. But it wasn't just the shoes. The whole package put her in a league of her own. Bill could feel the eyes in the restaurant flit by them, stop, then flit on, trying to be discreet, but hard to do in the small, intimate restaurant. In Chicago he had enjoyed the attention she drew. He felt awkward about it now.

He ordered the poached trout for Brenda, a New York Strip for himself. Then he sat back and waited for Brenda to take over.

Taylor sat back in her chair, across from Jack and Sue. Paul and Chris were to her right, Kent to her left. She had a half smile, half frown on her face as she watched the soap opera happening in front of her.

The boys had been drinking a significant amount of beer, and the two twelve packs were down to the final few. Jack had his arm slung over Sue's chair, his back partially turned away from Kent. Kent had the "deer in the headlights" look on his face, Taylor wasn't sure if it was the beer or the scene unfolding in front of him.

The evening had begun innocently enough. Laughing about the Nut Lady and the popcorn vendor's feud, the missing left turn in the directions that caused the butterfly garden followers to circle a block indefinitely, rolling their eyes over the tourists ordering Bass Waffles and expecting a Bayfield Bass cone, or vice versa. On this one Taylor got serious.

"Do you think that's a problem? That people don't know what they are ordering or what they are going to get? I don't want unhappy clients, and my marketing classes would say the branding has to be crystal clear…"

Sue defended Taylor, "You can't cure stupid, you know."

"Yeah, you can't cure stupid," Jack repeated. And took another swig from his beer.

"And you have pictures on the menu," Paul pointed out.

"Yeah, you have pictures," Jack said. He looked at Sue for affirmation. Sue could have been a poker player at that moment.

"Even I know the difference from the pictures," Chris piped in.

"Yeah, Me, too." Jack said. "Bayfield Waffles have ice cream and Bayfield Flaffles are fish with goo inside," Jack proclaimed to the group.

Everyone roared with laughter. "OK, we're cutting Jack off!" Taylor said with authority. And I'm going to work on my branding issue, with or without all of you!"

Bill finished the last bite of his NY Strip, and Brenda was pushing around the last few bites of the trout. "That was delightful, Bill. I'm amazed a restaurant like this exists in this podunk town of yours," she declared. "Now I'd like an after-dinner drink so we can talk about Father."

Bill ordered a Grand Marnier Cordon Rouge neat for Brenda. Black coffee for himself. He figured he needed to be alert for whatever Brenda was going to pitch him.

The waiter silently placed the digestif before Brenda, with an imperceptible flair. When he served up the black coffee, Bill was reminded of an old coffee commercial where guests in a high-end restaurant were served instant coffee. The waiter left, Bill leaned back, crossed his right ankle over his left knee, and said, "So, what did you want to talk about?"

Brenda leaned forward, self-aware enough to know her generous cleavage gave Bill reason to pause. "Mother and I need your help. You've worked with Father. You know how he thinks, and he trusts you. He's making changes to his will, and we aren't privy to what's happening," she said, all pretenses dropped.

Bill's interest perked up. He knew his father-in-law Rex had a first love—work—but his second was his wife and only daughter, on whom he doted. "What makes you think anything is happening that isn't in your best interest? Or your mother's? My experience with your father is that you're the center of his universe. Or at least one of the major planets orbiting around his work."

Then Brenda dropped the bombshell. "He was having an affair. With his administrative assistant. Mother is devastated. I can't imagine, that mousey little hussy…" Bill couldn't help but see the parallels, even if Brenda chose to ignore them.

"Well, Brenda, it seems to me you don't need an ex-husband's help, but a good attorney," Bill replied.

"Of course, we know that, and we've already taken steps to procure a good one that isn't already beholden to Father. But we need someone who can talk to him, you know, man-to-man. I can't do that. Neither can Mother." Brenda took a deep breath. It was hard for her to beg. "But you can. You have, ah, perspective.

"Please, Bill. We need you." Bill had moved his hand from his knee to the table, playing with his coffee cup. She put her perfectly manicured hand on his. "Please."

What man—or woman—can resist the pull of being needed? Not Bill. Not on this night of low lights, a fine meal, fine wine, a beautiful woman. And two years can dim the visceral pain of betrayal.

Bill uncrossed his legs, leaned forward, and as his lips met Brenda's, he murmured, "Of course I'll help."

Back to Bayfield

Chapter 19

The pig had been roasting for hours, looking mouth-wateringly good with the apple in its mouth and its skin a crisp golden brown. By the time Taylor got off work on the 4th, the pig was down to bones. She got in line and piled food on her plate: pulled pork, beans, potato salad, mystery Jello salad with marshmallows, and chips. A selection of desserts was set out, and she figured she'd go back for those. She looked around and saw Bill and Brenda at a table with Sue and Kent. She desperately scanned the other tables for familiar faces to sit with, but then Bill saw her and waved her over. She was caught and had no alternative but to join them at their picnic table.

Bill rose when she approached. Brenda was on his left, he offered Taylor the seat to his right. Kent and Sue were sitting across from them. "Taylor, here, set your plate here," he said nervously. "Taylor," he repeated, "I'd like you to meet Brenda. Brenda, this is Taylor Clarke. Taylor owns and operates Cool Creams and Berries on Rittenhouse."

Brenda remained seated but extended her hand. "Brenda," she repeated. "Boyt." she added, twisting the knife into Taylor's gut. "So nice to be introduced. I can't imagine how we haven't bumped into each other yet, the town's not that big."

Taylor smiled and shook Brenda's offered hand. She said, "You might not remember, but I was at the shop that you stopped at to ask where to find Bill. That was Bayfield Cool Creams and Berries." She said this all while imagining smearing Cool Creams all over Brenda's perfectly coifed and curled hair, over her lovely fair skin that contrasted so nicely with her dark hair. Taylor was suddenly conscious of her worn and stained Cool Creams T shirt and the three-year-old cut-offs that she had thrown on 12 hours ago. *I should have changed after work before coming down here,* she said to herself. Her hair was pulled back into a ponytail that stuck out of the loop at the back of her baseball cap. And if any of the make-up she had applied in the morning was still on, it was probably melted down to her chin after working all day. *Oh, well,* she thought. *Oh, hell.*

She sat next to Bill, greeted Sue and Kent, and looked over at Brenda's plate. There was a dab of pulled pork, a pile of green salad, and a celery stick. She watched as Brenda pushed the meager helping around her plate. *Eating disorder,* thought Taylor as she proceeded to dig into her plate. Taylor had never realized how physically demanding the food service business was. Aside from scooping ice cream into fragile waffles, she was constantly lifting, bending, and moving food, boxes and plates around the shop. On top of that was the work of washing berries, whipping cream and then blending the whipped cream with flavors to create Cool Creams. She ate heartily until she saw the bottom of her plate.

They talked about the business at Cool Creams and the steady flow of customers.

It had been a big day for Sue, too. She had been on the phone with the pyrotechnics company in charge of the night's fireworks and dealing with the wrap up of the vendor fair, farmer's market, butterfly garden tours and ongoing scavenger hunt.

Taylor went back to the dessert table and eyed the brownies, chocolate chip cookies, frosted cake bars, strawberry rhubarb pie and wild berry crisp. She had a penchant for chocolate, but her real love was the crisp on a berry crisp. "Hi, Mrs. Wilson. I always love your berry crisps. I'll take a scoop of that with ice cream, thank you very much."

Mrs. Wilson handed her the paper plate heaped with the juicy purple and ruby red berries and crunchy oatmeal, butter and brown sugar crisp topping. "Here you go, my dear. I gave you a little extra, I know how hard you've been working. Enjoy!" Taylor grabbed the plate with both hands to keep it from folding under the weight of the crisp and ice cream. She turned and began weaving through the tables back to where Kent, Sue, Bill and Brenda were still sitting. Brenda caught her eye, and purposefully put her right arm on Bill's shoulder, her hand reaching around his head to his right ear. Taylor stopped short, shocked at this display of affection.

A young man bumped into her back. "Oh! Sorry! Didn't see you stop! Pardon me," the young man exclaimed. Like in slow motion, Taylor saw Bill putting his hand on Brenda's, then she looked down in time to see the wild berry crisp and ice cream hit her chest from the force of the impact she took from behind. It happened in a split second. When she looked up again, Bill was standing up looking at Brenda, Brenda was standing up looking at her. She stood stock still, ice cream and crisp dripping from her chest, and stared at Brenda.

Then time began again. Bill turned to look where Brenda was staring and saw Taylor. He grabbed a handful of napkins from the table, and within three strides was in front of her, smearing the berries and ice cream around the front of her shirt. The young man who had bumped her was also mopping her chest.

"Wait, wait, guys. Enough! You're going to get a lawsuit with all your helpfulness. I'm fine, really," she said. "Oh my gosh, this is going to stain like mustard from a hot dog. All that good crisp gone to waste, too," she lamented as she looked down to see her white tennis shoes (which weren't so white after a day of work) splattered with red and blue berry sauce. She looked into Bill's eyes, wondering what he must be thinking and feeling; she wasn't exactly sure what she was thinking and feeling herself. He walked her to the table where Brenda was sitting. Kent and Sue were turned looking at her.

"OK, I'm fine, nothing a little scrubbing won't cure, and it's an old shirt anyway," Taylor said. Brenda recoiled as though just being near might stain her white Ralph Lauren Polo shirt with the little horse on the chest, and pure white slacks. "Lucky it didn't hit anyone else, though everyone jumped back mighty fast," Taylor said ruefully. "I better head to the shop to find a change of clothes."

"Come with me to the Loon," Bill offered. "You can take that off and wear something of mine 'til we get to the shop, and you can change. I insist."

"I can take her," Kent offered. Bill just shook his head. He was determined to follow this through.

They walked towards the Loon just a few hundred feet away. "I'm so embarrassed," Taylor began, "But it had to be pretty spectacular to see." She chuckled under her breath.

"I didn't see it all, but you did draw a lot of attention, and that color blue matches your eyes, you know," Bill said, smiling.

"You didn't have to come with me. You could stay with Brenda. She didn't look too happy…" Taylor began.

"Brenda is never very happy." Bill interrupted Taylor to say. "Trust me, I needed to get away from her. I need to put some distance between us. She's pretty, but she's got something else going on, an ulterior motive I think it's called."

"You didn't look like you minded her hand on you just now," Taylor countered.

"What? Yeah, maybe it didn't look like it to you, but she's way too forward, and I had to remove her hand from me. Not where I wanted to go," he said.

They had reached the Loon. Bill led the way down below deck and pulled out a flannel shirt. "Here, throw this on. Put your T shirt in a plastic bag—there's one above the sink. Come on up when you're ready."

She gingerly pulled off the T shirt, careful not to get any more wild berry on her sport bra or shorts. She threw it in the sink and pulled on the soft flannel work shirt. It felt good and smelled of spice and wood. The plastic bags were above the sink, and she put the soiled T shirt into a bag. She figured she would have to throw it out, anyway, but it was easier to follow directions at this point. She thought about what Bill had said about Brenda's hands-on move. She realized that maybe she had read more into it than she should have.

They walked back together to the shop, where she ran upstairs and pulled on a red, white and blue tank top and threw a jeans jacket over her shoulders. She decided to change from the old shorts to a pair of capris. She brushed her hair into a French twist and surveyed herself in the mirror. *This is as good as it's going to get,* she thought.

She ran down the back stairs and almost straight into Bill. He was coming around the hall from checking the front room. She looked up at him and said, "I guess this means I am coming to watch fireworks on the Loon. But I don't want to be a third wheel, and with Brenda here, I'm really OK watching off the shore with the rest of the town. It's how we always did it, anyway. You just have to shoot straight with me. I don't want to get in the way of a big reunion or anything…"

Bill stood still, looking down as she spoke. He admired her spunk, her indomitable spirit. "There's no one I'd rather be with than you. I have some business to attend to back in Chicago, so I'll be heading out soon. In the meantime, let's enjoy the Fourth and worry about what's next when we have to. Deal?"

"I'm not sure what I'm dealing with here, but ok, Deal," Taylor replied. "No one knows better than you and I that life can change on a dime. It's like AA, one day at a time."

"I'm loving Bayfield," he continued. "How close we are to nature, the sailing, the town. I've grown to love the old house I've poured my sweat into," Bill said.

Taylor smiled and stepped in closer. Bill wrapped his arms around her. "Let's enjoy the fireworks, shall we?"

They walked back to the Loon from her apartment over the shop as the sun was setting the western hills on fire. They stepped aboard and found Paul pulling out wine and beer glasses. Brenda, not liking the rocking on the Loon, opted to go back to the Bayfield Inn, ordering Jimmy, the marina man, to carry her lawn chair. No one missed her.

Kent and Sue boarded the Loon, arm in arm, Kent wearing new Wrangler jeans and a red, white and blue plaid western shirt; Sue stylish in a blue and white gingham shirt over Carhart jeans. They carried a pan of leftover berry crisp from the pig roast. "This is for you, Taylor," Kent said jokingly. Taylor laughed and punched her brother in the arm.

Chris arrived with a bottle of champagne and a cheese charcuterie board that he handed to Bill. Paul came up with glasses that Taylor took from him. With his hands free, he and Chris embraced shyly, the Scandinavian Chris with the dark-skinned Paul. They made a gorgeous couple. Taylor leaned into them and said, "I didn't realize you two were an item. I'm sorry I was so clueless. But I am very happy for you!" Kent, Sue and Bill all nodded in agreement.

Taylor held out the glasses that Bill filled with champagne. They handed out the bubbly as the fireworks began to fill the sky. Bill wrapped his arm around Taylor, and they stood together under the dark night sky. He smiled down at Taylor, his arms encircling her and said, "You have touched my heart," and then he bent down and met her upturned lips with his. And they tasted sweeter than ice cream.

With the Loon rocking quietly, exploding lights reflected off the water; glowing faces turned up to the bursting colors and booming reports. Off to the north, the large Boyt home overlooked the water and the Loon; lights from neighboring homes twinkled in the night.

The blossoms of colored embers lit up the sky. 'Oohs' and 'aahs' resounded throughout the marina as the town of Bayfield celebrated the birth of the nation. The three couples stood on the deck of the Loon, their faces illuminated by the fireworks. The future held nothing but hope, and maybe a new wardrobe for Kent.

Chapter 20

Taylor woke feeling no headache, no swirling room, no question about where she was. She kept her eyes closed, thinking back on the evening on the Loon, surrounded by good friends and family, fireworks lighting up the sky.

I could die right now and be perfectly happy, she thought to herself. But she knew that wasn't totally true, either.

Brenda. The proverbial thorn in her side.

Kent was already in the kitchen, frying up scrambled eggs and spinach from the garden. As Taylor appeared at the door, Kent had the plate ready for her. "Eat up, you can't live off love," he said with a twinkle in his eye.

"I'm not at that stage, trust me, big brother. But I did have a good time last night. Did you?" Given they both ended up at home, on the farm, in their own space, would indicate the evening ended above board for everyone.

"Yep, all good. I will say I may need to get a pair of suspenders if I am going to give up my Key overalls for Wranglers. Those dang pants kept sagging all night."

"Maybe you need to put a few pounds on your butt?" Taylor suggested.

"There must be another way," Kent said thoughtfully. "But, yeah, I had a good time, and I hope we have many more. Who woulda thought, huh?"

"I gotta get to town. Lots of cleanup to do, and we're only halfway through summer. Yeah. Who woulda thought. You gonna come to town today?"

"Not sure, there's a lot to do here, too. The berries are all coming in at the same time, and I gotta salvage as much as I can. I'll stop in if I get downtown. Have a good one, Taylor," Kent said affectionately, letting the screen door slam behind him as he left to start his day on the berry farm.

Taylor savored the fresh eggs and spinach scramble, thinking about the evening before. Bill was all warmth and smiles, making her feel like a million bucks. Brenda was in her hotel room, so there wasn't that chaos in the mix. Paul and Chris, Kent and Sue were all easy to be with, enough familiarity to be comfortable, and enough of the newness of the relationships developing to keep everyone on their toes. It was one of the nicest evenings Taylor had had in years.

She washed her plate in the sink and filled her Yeti mug with coffee and headed out the door herself. She pulled the door closed without locking it, let the screen slam a second time, and jumped into her truck to drive to town. The rest of the summer waited for her.

Chapter 21

Sue Boyt was already waiting for Taylor at the front door of Cool Creams, two cups of coffee in hand. Taylor parked in back and walked the length of the store to open the front door. "Morning, Sue," Taylor said.

Sue hardly acknowledged the greeting, handed Taylor the extra cup of coffee and jumped right into why she was camped on the doorstep. "Well, Miss Brenda hit the road this morning. And good riddance. I hate to speak ill of anyone, but if anyone deserves it, she does. How can a person make four days seem like forever? Don't know, but she sure did. Poor Jimmy and Paul had to help her load up that frunky trunky car of hers and they couldn't get it all in. Bill's going to take some down when he goes. Will that woman ever leave us alone?" she asked no one in particular. "I had a swell time last night, let me tell you. Thanks for all you've done for me and Kent. You know your brother; he needs some prodding sometimes. Like with a cattle prod." Taylor pictured the old cattle prod in the barn, batteries supplying the charge when the two copper tips touched a cow's flank. She smiled thinking of Kent getting that jolt.

"I hope Kent's a little quicker than a cow, but, whatever," Taylor said.

The two women sat at the round table, coffees in hand, waiting for the waffle irons to heat up. "What's next on your agenda, Sue?" Taylor had already been listing "to do's" in her head, noting the trash cans that needed dumping, floors that needed a quick mop, fingerprints on the front door window. She had to take inventory and restock after the busy week. The list kept growing.

Well, we have to start planning for Labor Day, but the big deal will be Applefest in October. That's the showstopper-end of summer extravaganza. I've already got some ideas for new events that I gotta get a jump on," Sue said, already starting her own list of "to do's" in her mind.

The bell rang and Chris Kigan walked in with a can of cream. Right behind him, Paul strolled in, whistling a happy tune.

Taylor put on four Bass waffles, each with chocolate hidden inside. "OK, guys, I need your help. We have the Bayfield Bass Cones that are becoming famous in our little town. But the Bass Waffles are getting confused with the cones. We gotta change the name so they aren't so similar. What do you think we should call the Bass Waffles? We're brainstorming here, no idea is a bad one, and anyone who criticizes someone else's idea has to pay for his or her waffle. Got it?" she said seriously. "Ok, begin. What do you think a good name would be?"

The words flowed, Taylor jotting down the ideas on a napkin. Sue started with "Baby Bass, Mystery Waffle, Goldfish Guts!" The group erupted in laughter. Paul jumped in with "Bass Blobs, Bass Goo," and Chris added "Golden Goo, Goo Gone." Someone yelled, "Goo Gone takes sticker stuff off. It's strong stuff!"

Just then Jack walked in and heard "Bass Buns, Koi Kremes!" He said, "Whaa?" and was immediately shushed. Taylor shouted, "Yo-Yo's."

"Yo-Yo's? Why Yo-Yo?" Chris asked. Taylor said without missing a beat, "Because if you waffle you go back and forth!" Jack had a glimmer and yelled "FlipFlop!"

Everyone laughed. Jack, who hadn't a clue what was going on, had jumped right in.

Someone yelled, "Waffle Sandwich," then Waffle Wiches", then "Cool Cream Cakes."

Finally, Sue said, "This is fun, but I gotta get to the Chamber. I'll see you all later."

Jack squeezed next to Sue and asked "Do you need a lift? I can take you."

Sue just shrugged and said, "No, thanks. Gotta hit the road." And she was gone.

Taylor looked at the group with great affection. "Thanks team. You all are my board of directors. I'll take the ideas and think about it. You're welcomed to stay, but I gotta start checking things off my list, too."

She went to the back room and got the Windex and cloth. She started on the front door glass. One by one, the friends got the message and trickled out.

Back to Bayfield

Chapter 22

At the end of the day Bill stopped by just as Taylor was flipping the open sign to closed. "Hey, Bill! Welcome! Can I interest you in some strawberry ice cream?" Taylor asked cheerfully.

"Not today, and you know that takes some great self-restraint. You want to go for a walk?"

"Can you wait a sec? I smell like a giant waffle, and I don't want to advertise in quite that fashion. I'll be right back," she said as she turned to run upstairs to the apartment. "You can wait here or come upstairs and sit in the front room."

"I'm good here. I'll wait." And he sat at the round table.

Taylor skipped up the stairs two at a time, tossed her jeans and t-shirt in the laundry basket and put on a fresh Bayfield T, shorts and Hoka walking shoes. She washed her face, put on a layer of sunscreen, pulled off the hair binder and brushed out her hair. She was ready to go.

Bill stood as she came into the front of the store. She was struck by his elegant presence. Even dressed in an old polo shirt, paint-stained khakis and deck shoes, he looked so put together. What was it about him that made a person take note? He was relaxed, but alert. She could tell he was taking her all in with one glance.

"Where do you want to walk?" she asked.

"I haven't been up to the house yet, and I gotta check on the progress, if that's ok," he said. She nodded in agreement and led the way out the door. He followed, and then she turned back to lock the door. They turned right and went the short block to 1st Street. The turret of the Boyt family home was a beacon that drew them towards it. They walked in companionable silence. The sounds of vacationers offloading the Madeline Island ferry floated up the hill from the water.

Rick was working on the porch railing as they walked up. "Hey, Rick!" Bill called out.

"Hey, Bill. Taylor. It's going well, but it's been slow. It's hard to get any help. We're getting things checked off the list, for sure," he said. Responding to questions before the questions were posed.

"Sounds good, Rick. I wanted to touch base. I'm going to be out of town for a spell, and just wanted you to know if you need anything you can reach out to me or to Sue. Either one of us can get back to you," he said.

Taylor looked up at him. *Leaving town. He had mentioned that he had to get back to Chicago, I guess it's going to be soon.* She thought to herself.

She stood on the sidewalk looking up at the beautiful home, the facelift taking years off the aging house. Bill walked up the steps and continued talking to Rick. The words, *bathroom remodel, new kitchen sink, banister repair* caught her attention. There was a lot yet to do, but it didn't sound like Bill was going to be here for the duration.

Bill and Rick were going into the house. "Hey, Taylor, want to see the inside? We have to talk about the remodel, you can look around if you want," Bill called out. Taylor didn't want to look too enthused, but she was curious about what they were doing.

She climbed up the broad steps to the veranda. There was an oval beveled glass front door that opened to a large foyer. To the left was the parlor, to the right an archway where the curved staircase wound up to the bedrooms, she presumed, and just beyond the staircase was a living room with a large picture window showcasing the beautiful Lake Superior, marina, and beyond you could see Madeline Island. *Wow*, she thought. *What a pity to sell this showcase. But who could pay the utilities? I'd have to sell a lot of waffles to heat the house in the winter…*

They had opened the kitchen to the living area creating a modern space filled with old world wood. It was a perfect entertainment space. *Or a great space for a family to gather,* thought Taylor.

She was jolted out of her reverie when Bill reappeared from the back of the house where he and Rick discussed a bathroom remodel. "You want to see the upstairs?" Bill asked.

"Of course!" she said. *I might not have the opportunity to see the house again, who knows?*

As they climbed the stairs to the second floor, Bill said, "It was great fun growing up here. Sue and I used to roller skate in the hallways, and playing hide and seek was a blast. It's sad it's fallen into such disrepair, but Dad was never very handy, and he didn't believe in hiring help. And then in the end the cold, long winters kinda did them in.

"I'm going to end up with seven bedrooms when I'm finished. Some of them on the third floor were for the help back in the day." They turned left at the top of the stairs. "This room was Sue's, this one was mine," they walked a little further on. "This room on the end we used as a guest room." Just beyond the guest room was a second staircase, this one narrower and steeper. "These are the stairs to the smaller bedrooms upstairs and these go to the kitchen downstairs," he led the way up.

There were three bedrooms on the third floor. It was a hot day, close to 90, and yet the house was cool, even on the third floor. "I thought the rooms would be hot up here," Taylor commented.

"Yeah, one of the things Mom and Dad added was air conditioning just before they passed. Thank God, it would be ridiculously expensive to add now," Bill said. "Here, come to the end room, the view is great."

He wasn't kidding. The room faced the lake to the east and had a full view of the marina and bay. It was spectacular. "Let's go back down, I didn't show you the master suite."

They went down the narrow staircase and walked past the guest room, his childhood room, Sue's room. They kept walking straight into double doors that he pushed open.

The suite extended into the tower that was the striking feature on the east end of the house, and then continued to the back of the house on the north side. A family of four could live in this room alone. And if the view upstairs was spectacular, this view was epic. Large windows, fireplace, marble, hardwood, lush Persian carpets. But underlying it all was comfort. This was a room to be lived in, slept in, played in. Taylor felt a lump in her throat. She thought she might tear up. Something in the room touched her to the core. *This is absurd,* she thought. *Get a grip!*

The feeling passed in a moment, and by the time she turned to face Bill, she was composed. "This is really something, Bill. You find the right buyer, and they will be lucky people, indeed."

"Well, let's hope they have money, in addition to luck," Bill laughed.

"When do you think you'll be finished?" Taylor asked.

"Originally, we had planned on mid-summer so we could list, but of course that's not going to happen. Then I targeted Labor Day, but Jimmy was just saying he just can't source the help. So now I am thinking end of September or early October. I could rant and rave to push completion, but I know how tough it is not only to get help, but materials. And I want it to be done right. It's too fine a house to remodel it in a half-assed way. Pardon my French."

Taylor laughed. "I don't think "ass" is French, and you haven't offended me, anyway. Shall we head out?"

They called out goodbye to Rick as they walked out the front door and turned right on the sidewalk. It was a sultry evening, even with the breeze coming off the lake. They continued walking west until they came upon the old iron bridge and when they couldn't walk straight anymore, they cut south, then west, then south. They ambled the tree-lined streets, keeping the conversation light. They rambled about classmates, work, the summer crowds, the berry farm, the Loon. They talked about corporate work compared to work here in Bayfield, the pros and the cons. They came upon Rittenhouse Avenue and The Copper Trout.

"Well, we're back to civilization. I'm famished. Let me buy dinner, and we can continue our conversation over some food. And maybe a glass of wine," he smiled.

"Guess I can't resist a glass of wine," Taylor said. "And you know, I'm pretty hungry, too. You'd think working around food all day I'd absorb calories through osmosis, but I don't think it works that way."

"Allow me," Bill said as he pulled the door open.

Well, I guess I am going to eat at The Copper Trout after all, Taylor thought. *I'm not sure how I feel about it now that I know the last woman he had here was Brenda, but…oh well.*

Bayfield is one of the northernmost cities in the US, and summer nightfall doesn't happen until well past 9 pm. By the time Bill and Taylor stopped at The Copper Trout, it was still dusky, with pinks and orange streaks coming from the hills to the west. Taylor thought about her last-minute decision to change clothes, and even though she was dressed for a walk, she fit right in with the lake crowd, even if a bit casual.

They were seated in the window seat, fun for them to watch as people strolled by, strategic for the restaurant to have the couple front and center. "Are you going to be sailing back to Chicago? Is that where you're going to be going?" Taylor asked. She was never one to beat around a bush.

"No, it takes too long to sail, and I need to get back. I've been able to handle my business remote, but the stuff with Brenda, well, I gotta be there, face-to-face," he said, avoiding her eyes.

"I thought your divorce was final. Or are you reconsidering?"

"Oh, no," Bill said quickly. "No reconsideration, at least on my part. No, Brenda asked me to come and help with her father. He's evidently redoing his will."

"And cutting Brenda out?"

"No, at least I don't think so. I guess I'll find out. She thinks he's having an affair, and I suppose she'd know what that's about," Bill said ruefully. "I worked with him some and never took him for the type, but then I didn't think Brenda was the type, either. In retrospect, maybe I was a bit blinded by the dazzle."

"Dazzle? Of the dad or your wife? Don't answer that, I'm just trying to be funny. You still feel a responsibility to Brenda?" Taylor asked.

"I must. I'm going back to help. Maybe it's as much a feeling of responsibility to her dad. I always liked him. He was a straight shooter with me. And that's what I judge people on, how they treat me, not how I'm told they fit in the world. I'm a bit more transactional when it comes to people.

"Not to change the subject, but what are you going to eat? I'm sure talking about Brenda and her problems wasn't on the menu you had in mind," he said.

"And not unlike a man, the way to my heart is through my stomach, too. I'm famished. How do you feel about splitting a pizza?" Taylor asked.

"Fabulous. It looks like they have good ones here, and I haven't had a pizza in ages. Order whatever you want, I'm sure it will suit me perfectly, since I've never met a pizza I didn't like," Bill said.

"And I eat a lot of frozen pizzas, so a real homemade one will taste divine," Taylor replied.

They finished their shared pie, smacking their lips and leaning back in their chairs. Bill checked his phone, smiled and looked up. "I have good news. The lawyers have an agreement put together to start looking at Cool Creams. I'll forward it to you so you can start reading it and as soon as it's signed we can get started!"

"That is good news," Taylor said, a big grin on her face. I can't wait."

She lifted her water glass to Bill and he raised his. "To the future!"

The evening had cooled considerably as they walked down the street to Cool Creams. They stood together at the front door, Taylor uncertain whether to invite Bill in or not. "I'd like to come in, not to the store but to your apartment, but I leave early tomorrow, and I haven't packed yet. You know this has been really special for me, spending time with you. I hope you feel the same way," Bill said.

Taylor looked at him, a little quizzically, a little bit resigned to the state of their relationship. *Friends. No benefits,* she thought. "I'd love to have you come in," she said aloud. "But I totally understand. It's been a special summer for me, too." *That kiss on the 4th of July must have been—what—a mistake? A fluke? It's like he's gone missing.*

It sounded like empty platitudes to her ears. Bill bent down, gave her a peck on her cheek, that, as she turned, brushed her lips. Awkward.

"Night," she said.

"Night," he responded. And he turned and walked down the street.

Chapter 23

Bill left on a one-way ticket back to Chicago the following day. Taylor didn't see him before he left. She had taken the agreement to a lawyer in town, after reading it thoroughly herself. She planned on signing it as soon as she had a legal review done, and within two days she had signed the document and emailed it back to Bill's office. Their research into Cool Creams began shortly after.

The summer tourist season was in full swing, and Sue took charge of the Chamber. Paul continued to stop at Cool Creams in the morning along with Sue and Chris and it became the morning ritual before each workday. Several weeks passed, lulling the group into a easy routine.

The bells on the door to Cool Creams chimed as Chris and Paul walked in. "Morning," they called out in unison.

Taylor came up front and began pouring Bass Waffles. "I have an idea on how to name the Bass Waffle so it won't be confused with the Bayfield Bass Cone. I'm going to put up tip jars on the counter, one of them will have FLIPFLOP WAFFLES and the other will have WAFFLE WICHES and whichever has the most money by Labor Day will be the new name. What do you think?" she asked the guys.

"Sounds fun," Chris said.

"Yeah, sounds fun," echoed Paul.

Just then Sue came through the door, catching the end of the conversation.

"Ok, you guys, what's going on? You aren't talking like anything is fun. Spill it," Sue said. She eyed them suspiciously.

"We were just talking about the name of the waffle again," Taylor offered. "And I am sure we were going to be talking about Bill, too."

"That Bill, he runs back to help Brenda, but he might be running from Bayfield, too. I think he enjoyed himself more than he thought he would here, and the house has really ignited some enthusiasm in him that I haven't seen in a while. It may not be the only thing that's sparking his interest," Sue commented.

"Mmmm," Taylor murmured. "I get texts from him occasionally, but that's about all. What do you hear about Brenda's dad?" She addressed Sue.

"Nada. I don't think he's dead yet. All that worry about getting their fair share. You'd think they might want to get a job," Sue said.

"What's going to happen to the Loon?" Taylor asked.

Paul answered, "It will stay docked at the marina. We will either have to come back for it or get it pulled out of the water here. Bill didn't say what he wanted to do."

The bell rang at the door and the morning breakfast crowd began. Taylor's waffles were becoming local favorites instead of ordinary donuts.

"I think I'm going to have to get a coffee machine soon," Taylor said to the room at large. And she began making her largemouth bass for cones.

Business slowed down around noon; Taylor figured people were eating real food about then. She sat down at the round table to take a load off her feet, mentally tallying up the morning sales, and scoping out the tip jars. They were even so far.

The bell rang and Demaris from Apostle Islands Booksellers next door walked in with a guy in tow. "Hey, Taylor! I'd like you to meet the new guy in town. Tom, this is Taylor. Tom is up for the rest of the summer, and he hasn't had one of your Bayfield Bass cones or waffle thingies. I told him he had to try 'em. And here we are!"

"Welcome, Tom! What's your weakness? A Bayfield Bass which is a whipped cream or ice cream cone, or a Bass waffle filled with strawberry, chocolate, or caramel. Or you can try them all," Taylor said with a smile.

"I've gotta run. I'll leave you in Taylor's competent care. See ya later, Tom, Taylor," Demaris called out. And the door closed behind her.

"I'll have one of those waffle thingies, with chocolate, please. And maybe one with strawberry, too. They're small," he winked.

"Comin' right up. Take a seat while you wait, it won't take long, but we cook 'em fresh, so it will take a few." She took note of his broad shoulders, fisherman's beard, wire rimmed glasses. He had on a Caribbean print short sleeved shirt, khaki shorts and flipflops. He carried a couple books under his arm. "How long have you been in town?"

"Not long, a few days, actually. I've been up a few times years ago. I needed a quiet spot to do some writing…"

"Oh! Are you an author? What do you write?" Taylor asked.

"Yes, I do some writing. Mostly up north murder mysteries, you may have heard of my detective? Gloria Rose? She solves all my mysteries."

"Sorry, I haven't been reading as much as I would like since moving back home. Most of what I read is what my book club in the Cities is reading. And we don't do many murder mysteries," Taylor said. "Doesn't mean I won't read one, though. You never know."

Here's your Waffle Thingy. If you'd like to help me rename these thingies, put your tip money in the jar you like: FLIPFLOP WAFFLES or WAFFLE WICHES. I'm afraid Waffle Thingies isn't one of the choices," Taylor laughed. "Though it might be a good backup name."

She handed him the FlipFlop/Wiche and their hands touched. *Wow, what was that? I could feel that touch all the way to my toes!* Her eyes followed him to the corner table by the window. He pulled out a book and began reading as he grabbed the first waffle. *He is one attractive guy. Slow down, honey. He just ordered a waffle. Not an engagement ring.* She laughed to herself and went to the back room to pull out more flavored whipped cream, then busied herself behind the counter.

"Hey, Taylor, would you happen to have a cup of coffee?" he asked.

"Sorry," she shook her head. "I've been thinking of adding that to the menu, just haven't gotten around to it yet. I think I'll speed up that process."

"Not to worry. I'm just thinking how good a cup would be right now. These FlipFlops are good. I like the chocolate, but that's just me. I'll be back for more," Tom said as he got up. He tossed the paper waffle tray into the garbage, gave Taylor a quick wave, and went out the door.

Back to Bayfield

Chapter 24

Taylor ordered a commercial coffee brewer that had a hot water dispenser on the front. She got an electric hot water kettle where she could heat up milk and began experimenting with hot chocolate recipes. It could be a good product extension with winter coming. Sue came in a couple days a week to relieve her for a longer lunch and that was when she would do research on new products to carry, advertising, social media and reading in general.

Tom began coming in on a regular basis. He would order one chocolate FlipFlop/Wiche and read in the corner. Some days he would have his computer and he would spend the hour or two writing. Every day he came in, Taylor would sit with him for a few minutes.

"How are you enjoying Bayfield? It's been an unusually fine summer, don't you think? Have you taken the ferry to Madeline Island yet?" Taylor asked.

"This is a wonderful community. I've enjoyed it very much. And Demaris has been so welcoming, as well as yourself. I appreciate your hospitality."

"I haven't been back that long myself, actually," Taylor said.

"Really? I was under the impression you had lived here all your life—Demaris had said you had a brother who owns a berry farm?"

"Yes, Kent has the berry farm, this storefront was my grandmother Emmy's creamery back in the day. I did grow up here. I was down in the Twin Cities for several years, working for Target. Got back here this past late winter and decided to start this business. The town grows on you, doesn't it? I mean, the people make the place, but the place—it's gorgeous. Have you been out on the water yet? That's when you'll lose your heart to the place," Taylor gushed.

"I haven't been out on the water. I don't have a boat, although I suppose there are rentals. What would you suggest, Taylor?" Tom focused on her.

"I'd kayak. There are some caves just to the north that are amazing. And there are guided tours that make it easy the first time you go. I'd love to show you that area if you'd like?" Taylor paused. "And anyone else who you want to invite?"

"No, only be me, and I'd love to take you up on the offer," Tom said.

"It would have to be next Monday, you know I work all the time, but Mondays I can get some help in. Geeze, I would love to go out, too. It's been ages."

"I can pick you up here on Monday. What time?" Tom asked.

"We should start early, it's less windy early in the day. I'd say around 8 am. I think the cliffs off Meyers Beach would be best and I'll take care of renting the kayaks and the tour. You won't regret this. It's fabulous!"

"Sounds like a date. Thanks, Taylor. I look forward to it. See you for sure on Monday morning here, if not sooner!" Tom said. "I can bring a picnic if you'd like."

"Perfect," she said. *Perfect,* she thought.

Chapter 25

The weekend was busy with end of summer tourists trying to get their vacations in before Labor Day Weekend. Taylor had a high school student helping, but her availability would end after Labor Day. Business would slow considerably after the holiday weekend, too. She was heads down at work all weekend. Chris Kigan stopped in, but when he saw the line for cones, he just waved and mouthed, "I'll come back later," and went back out the door.

So, when Monday arrived, Taylor was definitely ready for a change of pace. She was waiting at the front door, water shoes, rasher long sleeved shirt and a pair of khaki quick drying pants over her swim suit. She wore her wide brimmed hiking hat, too, knowing how intense the sun could be even towards the end of summer.

When Tom arrived, she had a Flipflop/Wiche ready for him. "Ah, the problem with going out with a woman who owns a waffle shop is that the waistline is commensurate with the number of waffles eaten to impress the owner," he laughed. Her heart skipped a beat when he had said 'going out with a woman' but she stayed neutral as she threw her duffle bag in the backseat of his Toyota RAV.

They drove up to Red Cliff and then continued on Highway 13 to Meyers Beach. Meyers Beach is the capstone of the Apostle Islands National Lakeshore Mainland Sea Caves. As they got closer, Taylor got more excited. "You're going to love this, Tom. I haven't been here in years, and I can't wait! I feel like I'm fifteen again!" Taylor had contacted the kayak tour company and made reservations. They had the kayaks, paddles, life vests and tour guides ready and waiting for them. Tom and Taylor joined a group of other kayakers on the tour, a ragtag group, some clearly had been kayaking before, some looking a bit jittery. Everyone was excited.

"By the way," Tom said, "I can't swim."

"You're kidding, right?" Taylor asked, surprise showing on her face.

"No, just never learned. I was more of a bookworm type, didn't go to the city pool like the other kids. But don't worry, as long as I have a life vest, I'm pretty comfortable on the water," he said. "And I mean 'ON' the water, not 'IN' the water."

"Well, I was a lifeguard at the pool when I was sixteen, so I can haul you back to shore if I have to," Taylor said, thinking how she might like to put her arm around him in a swimmer's rescue position. *What am I thinking?*

True to form, the waters were calm this morning, and the group got split in two. Taylor and Tom stood in the circle, listening to the safety speech, and then leaned in when the guide began talking about where they were going to paddle and then what they would see. Taylor had chosen the shorter tour, not knowing what Tom might like. She felt like it would be better to leave wanting more than over-doing it the first time.

She stood beside Tom, feeling rather than seeing his excitement, his openness to a new experience, his energy focused on the task at hand. She liked what she felt. She liked what she saw, too. Tom was an intense listener. He didn't take his eyes off the guide, absorbing every bit of information like his life depended on it. And in a way, it did.

Lake Superior can be treacherous, and many lives have been lost in her waters. The most famous shipwreck, the Edmund Fitzgerald, had sunk in 1975 and was made famous by Gordon Lightfoot not long after. The ship and entire crew were lost to the waters of Lake Superior.

Taylor was only half listening; the other half was focused on Tom. He was medium height, broad shoulders, not slim like Bill, but more of a build that would be comfortable in an easy chair with a pipe and book in a dimly lit coffee shop. Kinda like the Apostle Island Booksellers atmosphere. Suddenly she realized what the attraction was; he reminded her of Mike, her husband. Who had been dead now for several years.

She didn't mention this to Tom, who was struggling with his life vest. She stared at him, feeling a constriction in her chest. It was a cruel prank. *Let it go,* she said to herself. *Let it go.*

The group got on the water and Taylor said to the guide, "I'll be your last kayak and make sure everyone is keeping up. I've done this trip years ago, and I'm an old lifeguard. If it will help, of course."

"That would be great, Taylor. Appreciate the offer. I don't anticipate any issues, but it never hurts, right?" the guide responded.

The guide helped everyone into their kayaks, then explained how their foot brackets worked. He demonstrated a few strokes of the paddle, and then they were off.

Kayaking is a great upper body workout and core strength helps. Taylor was amazed at how easily it all came back to her, and how the work around the store had kept her strong. Tom led a more sedentary lifestyle, which also reminded her of her husband. They had done a lot of walking, biking, and hiking, but they weren't a pickleball or tennis couple. They were more of a "work" couple, a corporate power couple, which made his accident and passing all the harder to bear. Her wingman at work was gone, and it changed the dynamics of her career more than she could ever have imagined.

Tom was a steady guy and could easily keep up with the group. He lagged to stay with Taylor. "This is great! I am so glad you suggested it. I would never have thought to do anything like this on my own. Thanks!" he said warmly.

"It was as much for me as it was for you," Taylor replied. "I haven't done this tour in ages, and I think you will be amazed at how beautiful the shore and the caves are." She bumped his kayak playfully.

"Now don't go knocking me into the water," he laughed.

And then the guide began talking about what they were about to see. "On your right you'll begin seeing some cliffs and rugged shoreline. We'll be sticking close to the shore, don't worry, the water's pretty calm this morning, and we should have an easy paddle into the caves."

The sky was deep blue with a few puffy clouds. The water this time of year was warm but beginning to turn. The water was so clear the rocks on the bottom looked like you could touch them. Taylor's heart swelled at the view, the water, thinking of the man she was with. *How lucky can I be?* She thought.

They entered the caves, and the cool as they entered was striking. Luckily with the paddling work they were doing, no one in the group complained. It felt good to get out of the heat.

The caves were amazing; none they explored were so deep that they were ever in complete darkness, but clearly they had been carved out of a million years of water lapping against the rock. There were inlets and layers of colored rock that made up the shoreline. Pine and deciduous trees covered the tops of the cliffs, and the sweet tones of the birds could be heard out on the water.

They turned towards the first tunnel cave and paddled up to the cliffs. Then Tom could see the opening in the sandstone, weathered but wide enough to paddle through. He followed the other kayakers, one at a time through the mouth of the cave. The entrance was maybe 15 feet wide, the walls washed clean. He focused on the kayak in front of him as they wound their way through the narrow waterway.

Oohs and aahs came from ahead of them, and as they rounded the bend they could see why. The crevasse became a tunnel, and then the tunnel roof came lower and lower. One at a time the kayakers snaked their way through the spectacular network of caves, arches, openings, all the while looking up, down, sideways, at the ever-changing chambers.

Taylor had chosen the two-hour tour and everyone in the group was reluctant to turn to go back. Tom couldn't stop smiling. That made Taylor smile, too.

The dock came up to them sooner than either wanted. Tom slowed to be side-by-side with Taylor. "That was amazing, Taylor. I'm so glad we did this. And I am so glad we did this together, aren't you?" he asked.

"Yep, it was fun. And I had forgotten so much about the caves. I wonder if they go to different places every trip. Well, for sure this is one of those 'do again' adventures."

They loaded Tom's vehicle and stopped at some picnic tables at the visitor's center. Tom had brought a fine bottle of wine, cheese and crackers with blueberries and green grapes. He topped it off with a loaf of locally made crusty bread. They ate in companionable quiet for most of the time, then headed back to Bayfield. Taylor could feel the tinge of sunburn across her cheeks and nose--a result of having an indoor job and then spending all morning in the sun.

On the drive back to Bayfield, they were chatting comfortably with each other about the caves and the fine weather. She was about to ask him if he wanted to try to catch a movie on the weekend when he said, "My wife is coming to town this week. Her summer session at the University is finished, so she's going to spend the break up here."

"Oh, yeah? You've never talked about her. What does she do?" Taylor recovered gracefully. Internally she was mortified. *OMG, what was I thinking?*

"She's a professor at the University of MN. Her focus has been international business--she's amazing. You'll really like her," he said enthusiastically. "We lead independent lives, but she rows the boat, I've got no complaints. It allows me to write."

Chapter 26

Taylor couldn't shake off the mixed feelings she had about Tom. Her late-night texts with Bill and their occasional phone calls had kept her grounded, yet he hadn't made any commitments, even though it was clear they were attracted to each other.

She had found Tom to be attractive, too. Of course, she recognized the resemblance to her late husband. She found herself questioning her feelings for Tom. Why had she been so drawn to him? He never suggested anything more than friendship. But to have never even mentioned his wife? That wasn't right, either.

Each visit Tom made to Cool Creams was a reminder of her confused emotions. When Tom finally introduced her to his wife Stefanie, Taylor felt a pang of embarrassment. And then to find her friendly, open and engaging made her feel even more embarrassed.

"I love your shop," Stefanie told Taylor. "It's a great concept. Did you have help putting the marketing together? Is there an agency in town that you leveraged?"

"Actually, no, I pulled most of it together myself. I ran across these waffle irons in California. They come from Japan. The fish are called taiyaki, and the cones, well, I think the cones are just cones in the shape of a fish. Technically they're goldfish, but of course *bass* works better here. My experience is with Target Corp, so I have a bit of background,"

Taylor explained. "A friend of mine, Bill Boyt, is looking into franchise opportunities for me. What do you think?"

"My specialty is international business, I'm not an expert in franchising, but my gut would say it's got potential," Stefanie said. "Is that the Bill Boyt who's developed that internet marketing company that boomed a few years ago?"

"Uh, yeah. Do you know him?" Taylor asked, somewhat surprised.

"I think so," Stefanie replied "I was doing some work with the University of Chicago a few years ago. If I recall, he and his wife were at a U function that I was at. I think his wife's father was there, too. If I remember right, he's an alumni of the biz school."

I tried to imagine Brenda and Stefanie at the same function. Brenda, tall, model-thin, probably dressed to the nines, with a bevy of men around her. And then Stefanie: serious, smart, all business. Taylor imagined her dressed not as a model but as a businesswomen, with tailored clothes that had a hint of Asian influence.

"Brenda's dad heads up the Board of Trade. Was Tom with you?" Taylor asked. It was even harder to imagine both Tom and Stefanie at a function Brenda would be at. They seemed too… intellectual for Brenda.

Stefanie got a grin on her face. "Oh, yes, Brenda. Her name was Brenda. It seemed like such a down-home kind of name, and she was anything but. I'm trying to picture Bill Boyt. I can't picture him… I was there representing the Chicago Business School. Tom bowed out. He isn't into those kinds of functions."

She closed her eyes and tilted her head back in thought. "OK, now I'm getting his image. I don't see him alone, only with Brenda. Now that I think about it, I can't recall his face, but they made a striking couple. Both tall and slim. He made the perfect accessory."

I watched her intently. It was as though she was running a video through her mind's eye. She wasn't kidding about the accessory comment. I chuckled to myself. Despite the awkward beginnings, Taylor was warming to Stefanie. The woman was authentic.

Tom continued coming into Cool Creams, but Stefanie preferred spending her time at the bookstore. The only exception was early in the morning, when the round table at Cool Creams was the center of their universe. That was when Kent, Sue, Paul, Chris, and Taylor sat and planned their day. Occasionally Tom and Stefanie joined the coffee klatch. Sometimes Sue or Paul would update the group on Bill, sometimes Taylor would have the latest. None of it was enlightening, and everyone kept Taylor in mind when they fed back info.

"I heard from Mr. Boyt," Paul said. "He said a friend of his won the Chicago Yacht Club race to Mackinac Island. They spent some time together after the race in Chicago. They had worked together in the past."

"That Bill does like to compete," Sue commented to no one in particular.

"He's been that way forever," Taylor added. "We competed every day of our lives from Kindergarten to graduation."

Stefanie asked, "This is the Bill that I know from Chicago? The one we were talking about the other day? The internet marketing guru? Married to that Brenda person?"

The group fell silent. A few eyes turned to Taylor, but some stayed focused on their waffles.

Stefanie turned to Tom and said, "I think I just put my foot in my mouth, right?"

He surveyed the room. "Looks to be the case. Yep, I think so…"

Then Taylor broke in. "No worries, I think there's a lot of unspoken thought in the room. Full disclosure, Bill and I were classmates—Chris, too--and competitors all through school here in Bayfield. Then he went off to Stanford, I went to Madison. He came back earlier this summer, and we kind of got back together, but not quite. It's a long story. Of course you know Sue is his sister? I stay in touch with him, but he went back to Chicago to take care of business."

Sue cut in, "To take care of Brenda's business. They divorced a couple years ago. She claims her dad needed his help, but I think she has her own plan of attack." She looked pointedly at Taylor.

"Well, Bill can think for himself," Taylor said. Paul and Chris nodded.

"Sometimes if a person hears the same rhetoric over and over, it begins to seem like the truth," Tom said. "Sometimes a person needs to be reminded of the flip side of the coin."

Am I the flip side? wondered Taylor.

"I have a feeling Taylor can take care of herself," Stefanie said.

The tinkling of the bell at the door announced their first customer and the group began to disperse. Another summer day had begun at Cool Creams.

Taylor kept busy with the constant flow of clients coming to grab a Bass Waffle Wiche for breakfast or a Bass Waffle Cone for a cool treat mid-afternoon. She had plenty of time to think as she mixed, blended, poured, scooped and rang up sales. The high school girl she hired gave her some relief, but she was the proprietor and chief operating officer of everything.

At the end of the day, she felt fatigued but happy. She was exactly where she wanted to be. And during the hours at the shop, she had time to think of the processes she wanted to document for the franchising, and a plan of attack to get that job accomplished.

That evening, "her phone buzzed. It was Bill calling. "Hey. How are you? Busy still? Lots of tourists?"

"Can't complain," she replied. "Business is steady. Since Covid it seems like everyone is making up for lost time. And the kids run wild. Fortunately, there's not much breakable in the shop. But there have been a few up-side-down, on-the-floor Waffle Cones." She laughed. "How's your work going? Whatcha been working on?"

"Brenda's Dad. The guy has been running some of the family finances by me. Asking for advice. Talk about the tables turning. I used to sit at his knee and ask him for advice."

Bill continued. "The family is doing better. He was having an affair with a woman from his office. I don't think she knew much about his family life, though that's no excuse for him. He seems remorseful but Brenda's mom isn't buying it. I think he's pulled the trigger to end that marriage. She's not one to forgive and forget. More like 'has the memory of an elephant.' Isn't that the one that has a long memory? He offered me the chance to take over his finances and run the family office, but I declined. It's not my path." Taylor felt a wave of relief wash over her.

"What's a family office?" Taylor asked, her voice steady. "I've never heard of it."

"I hadn't either. It's basically the business of running a wealthy family's assets, staff, businesses, that sort of thing.

"Enough about me. What about you?" he asked.

"There are a couple new people in our circle. Tom and Stefanie. Tom's a writer, and Stefanie is a prof at the University of Minnesota. She said she might have met you at a function in Chicago a few years ago. I doubt that you'd remember," Taylor said. "I really like her, but at first I didn't even know Tom--her husband--was married. He's got that Ernest Hemmingway vibe. And don't ask me what that is, I'm not even sure why I said that."

"Um, do I need to get back to town to protect my interests?" Bill asked in a flirty voice.

"Depends on what your interests are, I imagine." Zing.

"The heat here in Chicago is building, I think I gotta get out of town. Still have some loose ends to tie up. I'm meeting with the team looking at franchising Cool Creams this week. They're finishing up their due diligence," said Bill.

He could have led with that tidbit, Taylor thought. Her heart took a skip. *What does it say about me that my heart jumps when I hear about the franchise opportunity, but only flutters talking to Bill? Am I reading too much into this?*

"Oh, and before I forget, I think you should begin documenting the work processes at Cool Creams. Things like recipes, how you do the work, what you do that's special for the customers, that kind of stuff," he added. "When you franchise, all that will be what investors are going to be looking for. And you will want to trademark or copyright the branding materials."

"Right. OK. Thanks. I've already begun thinking about doing just that," Taylor said.

"Hey, gotta go, Taylor. I'll call in a couple days. Miss ya," Bill said.

"Yeah, likewise," Taylor replied.

This long-distance stuff is for the birds, she thought as she disconnected the call.

Back to Bayfield

Chapter 27

During July Taylor stayed busy with the summer crowds that were steady and ready to take advantage of all that Bayfield had to offer. Taylor had gone back to the caves, this time with Tom and Stefanie, but the experience just wasn't the same. Maybe because the caves weren't so new, but maybe because her heart was in a different place.

One morning after the coffee klatch normally ended, Sue hung back.

"Things seem to be taking off for you, Taylor. I'm so glad business is good. No one deserves it more than you," Sue said. "I know you have been spending more time here at the apartment upstairs. I hope I haven't been the cause of that."

"Heavens, no, Sue. I like my privacy, and I love Kent, but I know I am encroaching on his space, too. He's never said anything, it's just evolved."

"Yeah, things evolve. Here I am, the town spinster, and I think I might be falling in love for the first time in my life," Sue said hesitantly.

"Well, Sue Boyt! I am so happy for you! It couldn't happen to a nicer person! And I hope the lucky guy is my brother?"

"Well, who else?" she asked indignantly, and blushing beet red, marched out the door.

That evening, Taylor texted Bill: **Got news. Appears Sue and Kent might be a thing.**

Bill replied: **Really? My sister Sue? Cool.**

Taylor: 😊

Bill: **BTW, sorry for being MIA. I thot I'd be back by now. Life got in the way. I'm working things out.**

Taylor: **I get it. Things are on autopilot here. You aren't missing much.**

Bill: **But I'm missing you.**

Taylor: 😊

Huh. Why is it so easy to flirt over the phone, but not so in real life? If I could figure that out, I'd write a book, Taylor thought to herself as she headed to bed.

Chris and Paul invited Taylor to go sailing on her next Monday off. She jumped at the chance.

"Hey, guys, thanks for the offer. I could use a change of pace, and to get out from behind the counter is a blessing!"

"No worries, we've been meaning to get you out on the Loon, time just slips away," Paul said. "Bill gives me a lot of latitude when it comes to the Loon. She's a beautiful boat."

"Even more beautiful with your attention and care," Chris said. "We all haven't had much time to talk, just the three of us. We want to fix that."

"What can I bring?" Taylor asked.

"Not a thing. We got it covered," replied Paul.

The following Monday, Taylor met Paul and Chris at the Loon in the Bayfield Marina. She couldn't help but think of the 4th of July on the Loon—fireworks exploding around her, Bill's embrace lighting up her night. That was then, this was now. Chris and Paul were hurrying about, getting ready to launch. They gave her a quick hug and told her to drop her stuff below deck.

She easily stepped across the dock to the boat, hauling her day bag and some snacks and a bottle of wine. She could tell Paul and Chris had sailed together before; their movements orchestrated as only two people who are comfortable around each other can be. She came back up and just stayed out of the way.

Paul was at the helm, Chris tossing the lines from the dock to me on the boat. He leapt from the dock midship and was on board as Paul jockeyed the large sloop out of its docking spot. The diesel engine hummed, Paul maneuvered the Loon towards the mouth of the marina, and soon they were out in the bay, headed north.

It was with a tinge of envy that Taylor watched the comfortable and coordinated way Paul and Chris worked around each other. She thought of that time, early in the summer, when she and Bill had been on the boat, working together, making the Loon soar. Like that day, it was perfect for sailing, the breeze crisp and steady, clear skies, the other boats keeping their distance.

They kept course northeast, staying in the channel between the mainland and Madeline Island. They sailed past Basswood and Hermit, then veered left between Oak and Manitou, towards their destination, Otter Island.

At the Otter Island dock, they took a break and anchored just off the Otter shore.

Taylor had been sitting next to Paul at the wheel. Chris stayed fore and at the signal, lowered the anchor. They stayed bobbing in the cove. Chris and Paul dropped sail, and as the activity subsided, the three sat around the pull-out topside table. Taylor had set out the bottle of wine and snacks that she brought. The two men accepted the glasses of wine proffered.

"Hey, guys, thanks a million for asking me to join you today. I really appreciate it. You want more salami? I can easily do that," She said.

"It's all good, Taylor. You can relax. We've got all day," Chris said. Paul just nodded.

"I know, but I like to pull my weight, eh? Taylor said. "I don't mind."

"We got you out here for a couple of reasons. First of all, we wanted to thank you for all your support. Ever since we met, you've been a great friend. It's been a factor, too, in helping us decide to make our relationship formal. We're going to get married this fall," Paul said quickly.

"And I'd like you to stand up with me." Chris straightened up as he made his request.

Taylor's eyes widened. "Why, I'm honored, Chris. Of course I will. I would stand up with you, anywhere, anytime."

Paul jumped in. "We're concerned about how the town will react. What do you think?"

"You guys probably know better than anyone how people will react. I wouldn't worry about the townspeople. You always have people all over the board about this stuff. And this town's pretty chill. How about your families? That's who I would be more concerned about," Taylor said.

"Yeah, you're right," Chris said. "I know Mom and Dad had kinda hoped you and I would get together. I never said anything either way. My siblings are all ok with us. Everyone has met Paul, everyone likes him. The little kids love him. What's not to love?" He reached over and touched Paul's arm and looked into his eyes.

"Well, you guys will work that out. I would love to help with the planning. Paul, do you have family that will be coming? Oh, I guess I assumed it would be here in Bayfield."

"Actually, we'd like you and Sue to help us with the planning," Chris said. "My folks are getting up there in years, and you two are the most organized women I know. Would you help?"

"Of course! Oh, this is going to be so much fun! I love weddings! Where will you live? What about your work, Paul? Chris, you need to stay at the farm, right? How will this work out for Paul?" Taylor's mind was racing. These were the exact issues she had begun thinking about for herself, in those 'what if' scenarios.

"To be honest, we haven't figured it all out yet. But we have time," Paul said and placed his hand on Chris's shoulder.

"I hope we have the rest of our lives," Chris replied.

Their glasses were empty, smiles touched every ones' faces. The waters of Lake Superior glistened as the sun rose higher in the sky.

The three friends continued chatting, their voices blending with the cool breeze coming off the water. Taylor spoke. "It's times like this I wish Bill were here. He's here and yet he's not, you know what I mean? His presence is everywhere and nowhere.

"I look at the two of you and I wish I could be as sure as you are about the future. My future seems… opaque."

Chris put his arm around Taylor. "If it's the right thing, things get clearer."

"I love my work. I love Bayfield. But I really don't think this is the endgame for me. I came here to get my bearings back after Mike died. That's over three years ago. And I can really say, now, after making the move and starting the business, 'I am happy'," Taylor said.

"That's great, Taylor. We all deserve to be happy, to live our best lives," Chris said.

"I agree. But I don't feel like this is it. I am thrilled to talk to Bill, he's helped me get through the summer. But I really get excited when we talk about the franchise opportunities, I think sometimes I must be crazy, to be more excited about an ice cream store than a guy, but it's true. I have visions of expanding. I can see Chicago, Minneapolis, San Francisco. And secondary markets, like Des Moines! I mean if we can make it here in such a small town with the tourist trade, we could make it anywhere."

"OK, maybe not Des Moines right away," the guys laughed.

"But Mackinac Island would be a logical expansion, for sure," she continued. And places like Ghirardelli Square in San Francisco, or The Pier in Chicago, or 50th and France in Minneapolis. Even locally, in Duluth. We could open a branch in Canal Park by the Aerial Lift Bridge.

"That's what made Mike and me so perfect for each other. Our work and our lives were intertwined. I want that again.

"That's what I miss."

Chapter 28

Taylor, Paul and Chris made it back to the marina slip by midafternoon. It was only the middle of August, but the days were getting shorter. Taylor left the men to finish tying off, and she walked the short distance to her car, threw in her bags and drove north on 1st street. The tourists were everywhere, strolling in and out of the shops. She turned onto Rittenhouse. It was even busier. Cool Creams, now staffed with the high school students, was open on Mondays. She knew that would change when school started and after Labor Day when the crowds would dissipate. But for now, she felt the glow of all that was good with her life.

That evening, Taylor had a Chamber of Commerce meeting to discuss Labor Day activities and the end of summer Applefest in October. She started going to meetings to support Sue, but it was clear that showing up also meant participating, and soon she was on several committees. Sue could be persuasive. But Taylor also knew what was good for the town and the activities that the Chamber supported benefited her business as well. Her Target experience helped immensely, but she also found her sense of the community and what would or wouldn't work from a marketing perspective, added value to the group.

Taylor was handed Sue's latest venture to get tourists to more businesses—the Bayfield Business Scavenger Hunt. It was Taylor's job to organize, promote and collect completed hunt pages for prizes to be awarded during the Applefest.

Businesses were eager to participate—especially not on the main shopping streets. It was always harder to get people to walk that extra block or two off the beaten path to a store that couldn't find space on Rittenhouse or didn't want to pay the higher rent.

Taylor enjoyed these projects. It helped her get to know the other business owners. She was amazed how many people she didn't know in the community. As a kid she thought she knew everyone.

As had become their ritual, Bill texted her to ask how her day had been.

Bill: **Long day. How was yours?**

Taylor: **Extra good! Went sailing on the Loon with Paul and Chris. They have good news. Not public yet. They are tying the knot.**

Bill: **That is good news. First Sue and Kent. Now Paul and Chris. Must be in the water. Have some other good news—I'm heading back, shud be there Fri. Want to talk to you about the franchise opp.**

Taylor: **Well, that IS good news. SYS**

Chapter 29

Taylor was back at the farmhouse in her old bedroom. She contemplated what she might take to the apartment in town. She didn't need much—she already had a bed, kitchen table, couch, armchair, and TV set. She went to sleep that night with a smile on her face. The franchise opportunity! Her head swirled with ideas. She thought about ways to improve, make things more efficient, yet keep the fun element in the shop. And she pondered how to do that as they expanded.

As she began to slide into sleep, her thoughts turned to Paul and Chris, Kent and Sue. And Bill.

She woke to the smell of bacon. It was heavenly. *Kent's awake. Can't take the farmer out of that guy. I'm going to miss this,* she thought as she stretched and contemplated another new day.

"Kent, that smells wonderful! Thanks for cooking," Taylor said cheerfully.

"Don't eat it all. Sue's coming for breakfast. And there's something I need to talk to you about. It won't take long." Kent kept puttering around the kitchen as he spoke.

Kent's proposal for Taylor to move to town didn't come as a surprise. "Sue's going to be spending more time here," he announced, "At least for now. No other plans yet." He avoided Taylor's eyes.

Taylor got up and embraced Kent. He looked down shyly. "I am very happy for you. Sue's perfect. And better late than never, right? I hope you will be very happy. I love you, Kent, and you have always been there for me. I am more grateful than you might imagine."

"I've been thinking about moving to town, anyway. I'll live in the apartment for now. It's more than adequate, and I'm not sure what the future holds for me. I am more than fine, and your support is part of the reason."

The idea of a fresh start intrigued Taylor. She was finally ready to embrace change.

Sue was arriving as Taylor was leaving for work. The two women exchanged hugs, and Taylor winked at her. "I told Kent that I'll be moving to town. I'll see you later."

Chapter 30

Taylor was the first one into the shop. She dropped her overnight bag upstairs and skipped down to start the day. As she got the waffle irons heating up, she began mixing batter and taking inventory of the ice creams in the display coolers. Using Kigan's ice cream saved her a lot of time, but it was expensive, and if she franchised, it was likely not viable on a large scale.

Paul and Chris came in the front door, with Kent and Sue not far behind. Taylor brought a round of coffees out, with a couple extra cups and began making Waffle Wiches for everyone. As Taylor finished up and everyone had their treat, the bell rang at the door.

Bill walked in, a big grin on his face.

All heads turned as he approached the group. Then all heads turned to look at Taylor, checking on her reaction.

"Well, Bill. Glad you could join us," Taylor said. "Pull up a seat and make yourself at home. I'll get you some cherry ice cream, or would you rather a Waffle Wiche?"

"Ice cream I can get most anywhere. I'll take a Waffle Wiche. So, have you picked the name? Waffle Wiche? It kinda rolls off the tongue. Hi, Paul. Chris. Kent." He went over and hugged Sue. "It's nice to be home."

Home. That's interesting, thought Taylor.

The friends around the table had a lively discussion. Bill had flown from Chicago to Duluth and rented a car. He surprised everyone, even Paul and Sue—and Taylor.

"A few things cleared from my calendar unexpectedly, and since this is where the action is, well, here I am," he said.

He had pulled up a chair next to Taylor, and got comfortable, crossing his legs. Left ankle over right knee. Elbow on the table.

"We just got here," Chris said. "We're glad you're here, Bill, so you can hear it from us, too. Paul and I are going to get married. We've asked Taylor to stand up with me, and also to help plan. We'd like you, too, Sue, to help us plan. We don't want to wait long. Now that we've decided, we don't feel like there's anything to delay us now."

Congratulations went around the table, and the festive mood continued. Taylor asked, "How many people do you expect to invite and who will attend? That will kinda determine the venue."

"Our families will constitute the biggest number, and then us, of course," Paul said, looking around the table. "And so probably 50 people all told.

"And we're thinking the second weekend after Labor Day," Paul continued, looking at Chris. Chris nodded.

"Well, by then my Waffle Wiche or Bass Waffle will be decided, but I think it's already leaning to Waffle Wiche. The whole town is calling them by that moniker already," Taylor said thoughtfully.

Sue jumped up and said, "Well, time's a wasting, there's going to be a lot to do, like getting a venue for one. Your date's after the summer rush, but it's only a few weeks away. I have some ideas; I'll see if they're available.

"Oh, there's nothing I love more than a wedding! Gotta go, See everyone later!" and Sue headed towards the door.

"Sue!" Kent shouted. "Sue, please wait just a minute, I think now's as good as any to let everyone know, don't you?"

Sue turned and stood uncertainly, then walked back. "Yeah, I s'pose you're right.

"You go ahead," she said to Kent. She stood behind his chair.

"Well, we aren't doing anything as drastic as Paul and Chris, but, well, me and Sue are going to try working together as a couple," Kent said.

"Hey, I need some clarification—maybe because I just walked in, but when you say, 'working together' do you mean 'being together' as a couple?" asked Bill.

Sue was beet red, grinning from ear to ear. "Yeah, Bill, I think that's what it means." Another round of congratulations went throughout the room.

"I wish I had a bottle of champagne here at work, but I think it might be a little early," Taylor said.

"Why don't we all meet at Morty's for lunch and we can celebrate?" Kent said.

"How about around 5, so I could close up a little early and not have to worry about coming back?

"You know, work never ends and all that," Taylor said.

There was agreement from everyone and the group stood up to go.

"Where are you planning on staying, Bill?" Sue asked.

"I'll stay on the Loon. If that's ok with you?" he said, looking at Paul.

Paul threw his head back and laughed. "Hey, man, it's your boat. I'm good."

Chapter 31

Bill sat with Taylor a bit longer after everyone had departed.

"I've got to go check on the house in a bit.

"Good to see you, Taylor. You are, as they say around here, 'a sight for sore eyes,'" Bill said.

"Why, what's going on?" Taylor asked him, wondering if Brenda was somehow back into the picture.

"I've got some business to discuss with Sue. I'll have to catch up to her, she left in such a hurry. Lots of stuff happening here in Bayfield," he commented.

"Yes, there is. You can catch Sue at the Chamber office. She told me she was going there today.

"Things working out in Chicago?"

"Yep, I think I told you I turned Brenda's dad down about the family office. I want to sever as many ties as I can with that family. And I want to talk to you about a couple things as soon as Sue and I can talk. Don't worry. It's all good," he reassured her.

"Well, you know where to find me, I don't venture far from here," Taylor said.

"Hey, how bout we take the Loon out late afternoon?"

"I'd love to, but I have to work today, and then we're going to Morty's, remember, at 5," Taylor reminded him.

"There might be time. It stays light a long time here. We can adjust." And he was out the door.

Taylor stood still, looking at the space Bill had occupied not moments ago. How could she be conflicted. He had it all. Looks, heart, job, money. But she knew it wasn't what he had. It was what she was building—her life, her longings, her future.

Nothing is easy, she thought. *And especially nothing is easy if it is worth having.* This she knew. She sighed and turned back to her work at hand.

Chapter 32

Kent was at the bar of Morty's for lunch anyway. He didn't want his good friend Jack to be blindsided when the news of him and Sue being a couple came out. He had his fried bologna sandwich and New Glaris Spotted Cow beer served up when Jack came in.

"Hey, buddy, couldn't wait for me?" Jack said. "Hey, Moira. Serve me the same stuff as Kent, please. But make mine a Leinie."

Moira just looked at him and nodded.

"Jack, pull up a stool. I've been waiting for you. Do you remember the discussion we had about the Memorial Day dance? And I called Sue and gave her a ride to the dance?" Kent asked, still looking into his fried bologna sandwich.

"Yeah, I remember. You were nervous as a cat, if I recall."

"Yeah, I was. But I've been calling that number ever since, and, well, 8224224 and me, well, we're thinkin' of being a couple; try things out, you know?

"You're my best friend, I wanted you to know before the rumors start up around here," Kent said quickly. He resumed taking a bite out of his sandwich.

Jack sat back, beer in hand. "Can't say I knew this was coming, but I am not surprised. That Memorial Day dance—I never told you but I called 8224224, too, but she turned me down. I've called that number a few more times. Still hadn't figured it out, but I guess it all makes sense now. She never had time for me.

"I'm happy for you, man. Just wish something good would happen to me, too," Jack admitted.

"Might not happen if you just 'wish' it," Kent said. "But don't ask me. I just fell into the honey pot, probably because of you, buddy."

"Uh huh," Jack grunted, and the two men sat side-by-side and finished their bolognas and beer.

Chapter 33

The day passed quickly for Taylor. Around three o'clock, the bell rang, and the door opened. Taylor turned, expecting more tourists dressed in tank tops and shorts, flip flops and sun hats. Instead, Jack walked in.

"Hi, Jack! Welcome in. What can I do for you? Bass Waffle or a Waffle Wiche? Name the flavor."

"Ah, I didn't come in to eat, sorry. I wonder if you have some time to talk?"

"Of course, I'll have my high schooler take over for a few minutes. Sit at the round table, I'll be right with you," Taylor said. She wondered internally what in the world Jack would need to talk to her about.

Taylor sat down, wiping her hands on her apron. "So, Jack. What's up?"

"Well, I don't know anyone else in town who might know about this stuff, and I don't know if you do either, but… I'm wondering if you would help me get on one of those dating sites. You know, like sweethearts.com or connections.com or whatever. I figure you're from the city, you would know how that stuff works…" he was looking down the whole time.

Taylor tried to hide her surprise. *Love must be in the air,* she thought. "Of course I can help, Jack. I am flattered you asked."

"I can't help right now, but tomorrow after work? In the meantime, it would help if you write down, or at least think of, the kind of girl you're looking for."

"Well, I know that already," Jack said. Someone like Sue. And since she's taken, someone else like Sue."

"What would help me is if you think about what it is about Sue that you like. Jot it down someplace, and then we can work on a profile," she said, putting her hand on his shoulder. "It can happen, Jack. Keep the faith."

By the end of the day, Taylor was ready for the celebration at Morty's. Her neck ached from scooping ice cream, and she was hot from the griddles. A cool one sounded perfect. The doorbell tinkled and she looked up to see Bill walk through the door.

"Hey," she called out.

"Hey," he replied. "I was in the neighborhood. Figured we could walk down to Morty's together."

"Thanks. Do you mind if I take a quick shower and change. It's been a long day, and I think everyone would appreciate me more if I showered.

"You can wait upstairs," She added.

She locked the door, flipped the open sign to closed. They walked through the shop, and he followed her upstairs. Her heart was singing.

Thirty minutes later Bill and Taylor walked back through the shop and locked the door behind them. Taylor was nervous. The last time they were together, the future looked bright. The fireworks of the 4th of July were like shouts of joy. But so much had happened over the course of the past month, she wasn't sure exactly where they were in relation to each other, nor was she sure exactly where her own heart was. What she was sure about was that she was very happy for Paul and Chris, and for Kent and Sue.

"I'm so glad you came back, even for a short stay. You know you are one of the topics of conversation at our morning coffee klatches at Cool Creams. Now that you are here, you can defend yourself," Taylor teased.

"I may need to be here more to defend myself. Ok, here we are. Ladies first," he said as he opened the door and stood aside.

Taylor walked in to find the key players already at the bar. She walked up, with Bill in her wake. "Hi, guys! Sorry we're a bit late. I had to close up, and I smelled like a waffle." She put a hand on Kent's shoulder, and one on Sue's. "Love you guys," she said, leaning between their tilted heads.

"Let's move to the table in back," Chris suggested. "I had them reserve one for us so we don't make too much of a ruckus up front here." They all followed him back, everyone coupled off, including Taylor and Bill.

They got seated, and Bill announced: "I have something to say. Sue and I met this afternoon to talk about the big house, and we've decided not to sell." A cheer from the group erupted. "The work is done; the house looks great. I'm going to move in and work remotely. Anyway, I've got the Duluth Airport within a couple of hours."

"Does that mean you're moving back to Bayfield?" Taylor asked, eyes wide.

"Tentatively, yes. I can work from anywhere, most of the time. I won't be actually moving for some time to come," he replied.

"Are you done?" Sue asked bluntly. The friends laughed. "Since Bill's not moving in for a bit, and even if he does, we thought the house would be the perfect place for a wedding, like for Chris and Paul.

"What do you think?" she asked, looking at the couple.

Chris was blushing, Paul's arm was laying across the back of his chair. "I was thinking of asking if we could somehow use the house, so this is perfect. Thanks so much."

The partying began in earnest.

It became clear quickly that sailing was out of the question. The group was going full swing, telling stories on each other, laughter erupting time and again. The evening fell, the light outside faded. It was closing in on 11 pm by the time everyone parted ways.

As the group disbanded, Bill walked Taylor home to her apartment. He reached to hold her hand as they walked.

"That was so much fun," Taylor said, looking up at Bill.

Bill was smiling, the corners of his eyes crinkling. "That it was. I am so lucky to have picked this time to come home."

"Yeah, you would have missed it all," she said as she opened the front door of Cool Creams.

"I know it's late; I hadn't planned to talk about this now, but if you could, I'd like to discuss the franchising deal with you," Bill said.

Taylor's heart jumped. "There's nothing I'd rather do," she said grinning. "I wondered if we were ever going to get to that."

"There's a lot to cover. Let's get comfortable. On the couch upstairs?" he suggested.

Taylor almost ran up the stairs.

"Would you like a nightcap? Or coffee, or water?" She asked.

"Maybe a water?"

"Comin' right up. Make yourself at home," Taylor said.

When she came back from the kitchen, Bill was stretched out on the couch, his feet on the ottoman, his hands clasped behind his head.

"Thanks," Bill said, taking the water offered. "Here's the deal: The franchise group wants to pursue the concept, and there will be a couple of team leads coming to take a look at your place. They think it's got potential. They've checked out the financial viability, and the scalability of the business. They can glean a lot of this going through the financials, but they want to get a feel for the intangibles of the business. That's why they want to come here. This would happen next week, and then we'll look at a 'package' for you, if it gets to that point." He pulled out his phone to check something. "I think I covered the key points I was sent here to relay." He smiled.

"Sounds good," Taylor said, thoughtfully. "But let's be clear. If your team likes it, they make me an offer—a 'package' as you call it. If I don't like the package, or if they don't like what they see here, then I am free to franchise on my own, or find someone else, right?"

"That sounds right to me. All the details were in the contract you signed when we started the due diligence part of the process," Bill responded. "Your experience at Target is shining through.

"And one other thing," Bill continued. "This is kind of sensitive. While we are going through this vetting, you and I have to be on the up and up. I'm embarrassed to even say this, but I don't want the investors to have any reason to think this is anything but a business deal. I hope you understand. It's a bit awkward, but necessary. OK?"

She looked at him carefully. Here he was, half inclined on her couch in the tiny apartment over the shop, telling her this could only be a business relationship. "Oh, yeah. I get it," she told him.

I love my business. The rest can follow. Or not, she said to herself.

Chapter 34

The franchise team had come and gone back to Chicago to write up their findings. *Corporate America,* thought Taylor. *Everything takes forever.*

While Bill was in town, Taylor took her Monday off and the two went off on the Bayfield Chamber scavenger hunt. It was partly work for Taylor, since the Chamber had charged her with the hunt; at each stop she was able to thank them for their participation. At the last stop, The Copper Crow Distillery, they both had a gin and tonic made from the Copper Crow whey-based gin.

"I've had some fine gins over the years. Of course, the Tanqueray's, the Hendricks, the Sapphires. I've had some of the best out of Japan that are not even well know except for connoisseurs. But I can honestly say I have never associated whey with gin. This is a first," Bill declared.

Taylor just tossed her head back and laughed. "Well, I can say this gin has the most unique flavor I have ever experienced. It's one of those, 'you had to be there' kind of experiences."

Her favorite times with Bill were the few sailing excursions they took together. One warm, late afternoon, Sue and Kent joined them on the Loon. Taylor played the perfect first mate. They dropped anchor off the southeast side of Madeline Island in Big Bay, and the four siblings sat in amicable silence.

Bill pulled Taylor up to her feet and with her hand in his, walked to the front of the bow, a couple pillows under his arm. He put the pillows at their backs, and they sat together, feet propped on the railing. Side by side, half reclined, they soaked up the sun, knowing the summer was waning. They could hear Sue and Kent talking quietly behind them.

"I'll have to head back to Chicago soon. I hate to go. The pace is so much slower here, even though everyone's busy. The season's about over and I have fires burning at the office to take care of," Bill said, speaking to the sky.

"We'll miss you around here."

"*I'll* miss you around here," Taylor said in a low voice. Bill grabbed her hand, brought it to his lips and gave it a soft kiss.

The spell was broken by Kent's voice. "Hey, hate to break up the party, but it looks like storm clouds forming to the northwest. Do you think we should head in?"

Bill sat up and looked. "Yep, we better pull anchor or we'll all be soaking wet pretty soon." And with that, the Loon made its way back to Bayfield Marina.

Bill had been good to his word. Except for some late-night movies and dinners together, he was the perfect gentleman, and she was the perfect potential client. They talked about business most of the time, the franchise opportunity for Taylor, Bill sharing information on other projects with her.

On his last night in town before heading back to Chicago, they were sitting together on her living room couch, glasses of wine on the coffee table, both leaning back into the soft sofa.

"Stefanie—you know, Tom's wife—mentioned a potential investor to me the other day. A contact she made through the business school. He might be interested in Cool Creams," Taylor said to Bill. "She's back at the University, teaching. I asked her to let them know you've got first right of refusal though."

"We should know soon the recommendation from the team assessing Cool Creams for us, and then the board will help decide. We have right of first refusal, but if it goes south with us, you know you're free to go out on your own.

"I hope things work out, though," Bill said, and took her hand. "On both deals," he added.

Taylor looked at him. "What do you mean?"

"Cool Creams. You and me. Two deals. Once the decision is made with the franchising, I can move forward with you. Is that too cold? To look at our relationship as a deal? I'm sorry, it's the analytical in me coming out. I don't want my feelings for you to affect the franchising team. I'm really trying to stay out of their way. It's got to be their decision, not mine. Does that make sense?

"Once they make their recommendation, and the board acts on it, I can move forward. Can you wait for me?"

Taylor took his arm and wrapped it around her shoulder. "I've waited a long time, I can wait a little longer," she said.

Back to Bayfield

Chapter 35

In September the days became noticeably shorter and cooler. It was like the switch turned on Fall in Northern Wisconsin. Students were back in school, tourist numbers dropped during the week. But the new draw for out-of-towners was the colors. Fall in the north was a glorious display of yellows, golds and reds. The leaves were just beginning to turn. Taylor had worked on documenting Cool Creams business processes and compiling the branding and product names she needed to trademark. She learned that she couldn't trademark or copyright Gramma Emmy's recipes so she was exploring trade secret law.

Paul was busy during the day preparing to dry dock the Loon for the winter. The marina equipment pulled the large sail and power boats out of the water with a specialized large lift that raised the boats out of Lake Superior and then they moved them to the parking lot for the winter. Water lines needed to be flushed, repairs and painting of the hull could be done on land, and the sails and lines would be pulled and stored for the winter. All the boats had to be out of the lake before the hard freezes came—in a few months Bayfield would become a frozen wonderland, with ice solid enough that an ice road would become the connection between Madeline Island and the mainland. And even though the water would stay open for a few more months, few sailboat owners wanted to be on the lake when the temperatures fell below 40. The cold winds of Lake Superior could chill a man (or woman) to the bone.

Kent was busy harvesting the last of the berries and getting ready for the apples that were ripening, and Chris was busy all the time—cows wait for no man—and the grain harvests and last hay cutting was keeping him occupied.

Sue and Taylor worked with Paul and Chris on wedding plans. The house looked spectacular, and the planning was going smoothly. In a blink, Bill was back in town. Taylor went to Duluth to pick him up at the airport and took him to the dealership where a red Chevy pickup was waiting for him. Their greeting was perfunctory, but warm. "Hey," was all Bill said in a low voice, as he embraced her at the airport.

As she drove him through Duluth, he reached over to take her hand. "This felt like a long separation, didn't it? And it was only a couple of weeks! I feel like a kid again," Bill said to her.

"Me, too," she replied, squeezing his hand. "I'll catch you up on the latest, and then follow your new truck back to Bayfield." They chatted comfortably on the short drive to the dealership, and then made their way back to Bayfield.

Chapter 36

The big event at the Boyt house arrived, celebrating Paul and Chris's union. The wedding was in the great room, the view of Lake Superior made a backdrop to the east, and the downtown of Bayfield to the south. Guests from the marina and Paul's Chicago friends and family, plus Chris's parents, his large extended family--which included a plethora of nieces and nephews--and one large and gentle Holstein cow, filled the yard and home with joy and laughter.

Sue officiated the wedding. Taylor wore a long black gown with white trim that mimicked a tuxedo. She stood with Chris, while Paul's brother stood up with him. A niece and nephew were flower girl and ring bearer; they all stood in front of the east facing windows which were bordered with fresh flowers. It was picture perfect.

After the vows, guests were invited to try their hand at milking the cow that was tethered on the front lawn, chewing on a bale of hay. More laughter rang out as guests dressed in their Sunday best, sat on the three-legged stool and clumsily squeezed the poor cow's teats. She just continued chewing through it all.

Sue and Kent wandered the gardens and ended up at the reflection pool on the west side of the house. "That was a right nice ceremony, didn't you think, Sue?" Kent said shyly. The evening glow cast warm shadows around them.

Sue, grabbing his hand, said, "Made my heart swell. Two of the nicest people on earth. It just seemed so right, didn't it?"

"We're pretty nice people, too. Maybe someday…someday soon…you and me? We could do something similar. Would you want to, Sue? Someday?" Kent asked.

"Maybe. Someday. Soon." Sue replied and gave Kent a peck on the cheek.

"But without the cow," Sue added. Kent just chuckled and beamed.

Chapter 37

As the night drew to a close, Bill took Taylor aside and they found a quiet moment together. Bill in a black tuxedo and Taylor in her tuxedo gown, made for a fine looking couple. Taylor wondered if Stefanie would describe one or the other as an "accessory". Somehow, she didn't think so.

"I just heard back from the franchise team and board. The deal is a 'go'. Legal is drawing up the papers, we should have it by Monday," Bill said quickly.

"Such good news! I am so happy, and so relieved. It feels like a long time coming.

"Thank you, Bill. It wouldn't have happened without your support.

"I can't wait for Monday! So much to do! So much to think about! Can you tell I'm excited? And not to be a downer, but even if it doesn't work out, I have learned so much, and it's been fun working with you and your team on this; it just adds to my arsenal of work weapons. I'm glad you see the potential in Cool Creams as much as I do," Taylor said, breathlessly.

"And I have decided to be the lead on the project—they code named it Waffle World—So you and I will be working together to make Cool Creams, a.k.a. Waffle World, a reality. You will be the Waffle Queen, and I," he paused for effect, "will be the Waffle King."

Taylor was grinning from ear to ear, her heart full. Bill leaned in, and gave her a long, slow kiss.

"What a wonderful evening," Bill said into her ear.

She pulled back and looked into his eyes and said, "What a wonderful summer."

Then she got a twinkle in her eye. She grabbed Bill's hand.

"Let's go milk us a cow!"

Epilogue

The days that followed were a whirlwind of activity. Bill began moving into his new/old home, feeling a sense of peace he hadn't felt in years. The franchise deal flourished, bringing the prospect of prosperity and new challenges that he and Taylor could face together.

Their relationship blossomed, rooted in mutual respect and a deep understanding of each other's journeys. Taylor realized that the years of grief had not only healed her but also prepared her for this new chapter. She understood how critical her work was, and how having a partner engaged in her work made her feel complete.

She learned over the past year what made her happy and what caused her angst. She was ready to commit, ready to embrace love and life fully.

As she looked out over the serene Bayfield waters from Bill's porch, Taylor knew she was home. Not just in a physical sense, but in her heart. She had found her place, her people, and most importantly, herself.

Bill came up behind her, wrapping his arms around her waist. "Ready for our next adventure?" he whispered. Taylor smiled, leaning into him. "With you, always." And with that, they looked east across the expanse of Lake Superior, and faced their future together.

Acknowledgements

Thanks to Bill, Sue, and Kent, for making my summer in Bayfield enough to write a book about! It couldn't have happened without you.

Thanks to my kids. They have never given up on me, and though each book takes forever to write and publish, they stay supportive and only roll their eyes behind my back.

Thanks to Theresa, Tierza, Ann, Richelle, Mel, Louise and Barb-in Heaven: My book club and best friends.

Thanks to the Kooks and Curious Minds Meet Up group in Santa Fe for all their support and friendship.

Thanks to my Sunday morning Shut Up and Write cohorts. How many Sundays did I feign writing because they held me accountable, and somehow work was produced.

Thanks to my Nikkei Write Now group, for the best craft sessions and great critiques, humbling though they may be.

And **thanks** to all the romantics out there, who still believe in love.

Other books by Elaine Koyama

LET ME IN a Japanese American Woman Crashes the Corporate Club 1976-1996

Solo Ski Sojourn
Solo Ski Sojourn 2

Musings of an Ungeisha

Contributor to:
Dust Up, an Anthology by New Mexico Writers, Jennifer Edelson, editor
Retreat2Write Anthologies, 1 & 2, Elaine Koyama, editor
A Farm Country Haying, Gordon & Nancy Fredrickson, Authors

Back to Bayfield

Coming soon, Koyama's long anticipated historical fiction about a young Japanese American couple navigating the treacherous socio-political climate of WW2 in Southern California. Here's a sneak preview.

Between Two Freedoms

Guadalupe, California, 1941

Mornings were cool until the sun burned off the fog that rolled in every night from the ocean. It was a typical morning in Guadalupe, California, a small farm town that was home to many Japanese who provided cheap labor for the vegetable farmers working the rich land along the Santa Maria River. My older brother Ben and I were waiting by the front door of our boarding house for Cunie Araki, our friend since middle school. Cunie exuded friendliness and good cheer—always upbeat and ready for adventure. He had taken me and Ben under his wing when we had moved to town, introducing us as Brains and Brawn. Ben was big back then, thus Brawn, and Brain for me was a way to explain why Ben and I were in the same grade but not twins. In truth, it wasn't that I had brains but because when we were five and seven, we had returned to America after two and a half years in Japan, not remembering a word of English. We spoke only Japanese. The school put Ben in the same grade as me to make it easier for him to catch up.

Cunie was our ride to the chili pepper sorting shed. I heard the quick "beep, beep" before I saw the beat-up old jalopy pull up and we ran down the steps. The back door opened, and welcoming smiles pulled me in.

"Good morning!" We greeted each other. Two girls were in the back seat, Margarita Kurokawa and Jits Hamamoto, my friends since I had arrived seven years ago at the awkward age of thirteen. My dad moved us from Los Angeles looking for work knowing there was a large population of Japanese immigrants living here. Margarita was tall and lank, with a long, narrow face that had an inquiringly raised eyebrow framing her dark almond eyes; We never knew if the eyebrow gave her the inquisitive, questioning personality, or if the inquisitiveness was a result of the raised eyebrow.

Jits was the female version of Cunie--happy-go-lucky, cute-as-a-button class clown, short and coiled like a spring ready to pounce on the next new party. And then there was me, Emmy Kubo. When I first came to town, I had the classic bowl haircut, but now I sported a perm, not so curly as Jits, but not straight like Margarita. I had a heart-shaped face with wide set eyes and a small mole on the right side of my chin. The girls teased me that it was a "beauty mark".

Tokio "Toke" Yonekawa, as serious as he was funny in a droll and subtle way, was in the front seat and scooted to the middle when Ben approached. It was good that Toke and Cunie were small in stature because it meant Ben could squeeze his big frame into the front with the guys, a sheepish grin on his face. His head began bobbing to the beat of the music that was blaring on the radio and we began singing to Glen Miller's *Chattanooga Choo Choo*. Jits was the loudest and had a decent voice. Margarita sang along but was tone deaf. Toke was a booming baritone and Cunie, ever the jokester, would honk the horn to the beat. Ben's bass voice matched his size—he was as big as the other two boys were small--atypical for a young Japanese American man. But like so many big men, Ben was a gentle protector—he was always looking out for me, even though I never felt I needed to be looked after. I was an alto in the choir and loved to sing. We continued like this all the way to work. Every morning was the same, giving us something to look forward to before the tedium of the day.

Cunie pulled into the dirt parking area next to the sorting shed, a small cloud of dust announcing our arrival as we unloaded--laughing and talking--Jits, Margarita and me, Ben, Toke and Cunie. Best friends forever! We knew we weren't going to work sorting chilis for our whole lives. After our graduation in 1939, Margarita had started at secretarial school, and Jits was attending a sewing trade school in LA. Toke was going to college in Santa Barbara. Ben had enlisted into the Army, his induction date in February. Only Cunie and I were at loose ends, still living in Guadalupe. I was looking into becoming a dental assistant, not because I was particularly interested in it, but because a dental hygienist had been nice to me when I had my infected front tooth pulled. But this was December holiday break, and we were all together again earning extra money during the busy chili sorting season.

We entered the shed doors, paused at the check in table and wrote our names and arrival times on the timesheet for the day: Sunday, December 7, 1941. Chili sorting was a seven day a week job—chilis ripen within days and there was no time to waste. Margarita, Jits and I joined a group of other girls headed to the sorting tables, all Japanese with some Filipinos thrown in. We all looked similar to each other—black hair pulled back, women and girls in colorful short sleeved shirts tucked into calf length skirts. There were about 45 chili sorters. Mother came in after us with a few other *Issei* (first generation) moms. We filed to long tables in rows, five women per table.

The shed was a wooden building, the sides made of large doors that could be opened, with a roof overhang to shade the interior. Our tables faced out so we could see the green crops that grew just outside the perimeter. The field workers were walking the rows, picking or weeding, or doing whatever their task for the day might be.

Ben, Toke and Cunie joined the other men and boys who would take the big crates of chilis and place one in front of each of us. We would take the chilis and sort them into three bins that were at our feet: the perfect ones went in the bucket on the left. The good ones but not perfect (either too big, too small, over-ripe but not mushy, red or green) went in the middle bucket that would go to the dryers and finally the third bucket that we tossed the moldy, over or under-ripe, stems, stalks, shriveled, unusable peppers that would go to the pigs or back into the field as fertilizer. The men would hustle to keep the women supplied with crates of fresh picked chilis, then empty the three sorting bins to keep the work flowing. Many of the men and boys were out in the field picking the chilis all day long. Chili picking was hot, mindless work, and the men had to fill enormous bins with chilis. The jobs weren't difficult—it was all just labor intensive. We chili sorters worked in the large shed, out of the direct sun, with big fans keeping us cool. There was plenty of time to talk.

Ruby and Sachi, younger than the three of us, joined at our table. Mother and her *Issei* friends were at a table several rows in front of us. Issei was the Japanese word for the new immigrants, the first generation to move to America. Most of the *Issei* couldn't speak English fluently, but they could understand a lot. Those of us born in the US were referred to as *Nisei*, or second generation in America. We all worked sorting the chilis—a never ending flow of reds and greens.

Jits would always start us on a topic—today it was about the movie we had seen at the Royal Theater last night. A group of us had gone to "A Night in Havana" starring Alice Faye & John Payne. Jits started teasing me about Cunie. "Hey, our little Emmy had a hot seatmate last night, yah?"

I blushed.

Margarita, in her somber way added, "Emmy can take care of herself. The guys, I'm not so sure…" They all laughed and I just kept my head down, sorting chilis.

"So, who sat next to you, Emmy? We weren't there! Let us in on the secret!" Ruby said as Sachi tossed a chili at her head.

I blushed again and looked away. "It was nothing, these girls are just teasing me," I told Ruby and Sachi. They were eager to learn from us older girls, and not just about sorting chilis.

"So, Emi-chan, who bought you that popcorn at intermission, huh?" Jits continued. She just never knew when to stop.

"For your information I bought it myself," I lied. Cunie had bought it for me but I wasn't going spill the beans. "And I didn't sit next to anyone."

I had wanted to, don't get me wrong. And Cunie came into the theater and sat next to me briefly. Then he got up and left. I didn't know why. At the concession stand I found him at the popcorn counter. I asked him, "Why didn't you sit next to me?"

He chuckled and said, "I wasn't sure it was you! It was so dark. And I had my sunglasses on." We both smiled. It was so like him to do something goofy.

But I didn't tell the girls that. I kept my personal life very personal. Jits continued, "Well, If I had a hunky man like Cunie wanting to sit next to me, I would be saving him a seat and telling everyone about it!"

Margarita countered. "Jits, you will never have a hunky guy wanting to sit next to you. But the bookworm types, well, that's a different story. You make them look smarter…"

We all laughed. Right then, Ben grabbed a huge bin of peppers. His muscles flexed under his light tan shirt. My brother would have been mortified if he knew we were all looking at him. Margarita said, "There's a reason I think Ben is the smartest man in the room..." She smiled.

Jits burst out laughing. "I wouldn't call that smart... but you can call it however you see it. He's a hunk!"

I blushed. He was my brother, and I can't say I protected him like he protected me. And he may have needed more protection than me. He was so timid. I looked up from my chilis and saw Margarita's eyes following Ben across the room. I loved her like the sister I never had but I couldn't help but feel sorry for her, too. Ben was so oblivious.

The radio was blaring, loud enough to be heard above the fans that kept the air circulating in the shed. Artie Shaw's clarinet *Frenesi* was playing and a few heads were bobbing to the beat.

"Hah!" Jits cried. "I'm not the one for bookworms! Damn!" she lamented as she picked a good chili out of her trash bin. "Give me a judo champ!" It was a dig at Margarita, as everyone knew that Ben competed in judo.

It was Margarita's turn to blush. I was ok with their chatter. It kept the attention off me, and I preferred not to be the center of attention.

The banter continued, back and forth, as we kidded each other. *Fools Rush In*, a Glen Miller tune, played on the radio. It was only Sunday, but we began talking about what we were going to be doing next weekend and what we were going to eat for lunch.

Then our chatter was interrupted by the radio announcer, abruptly breaking into the middle of a song.

"We interrupt our programming for this important message:"

REPORTER:

"One, two, three, four. [A reporter tested his microphone. The sound was crackly and scratchy.]

Hello, NBC. Hello, NBC. This is KGU in Honolulu, Hawaii.

I am speaking from the roof of the Advertiser Publishing Company building. We have witnessed this morning a distant view of a brief full battle of Pearl Harbor and a severe bombing of Pearl Harbor by enemy planes, undoubtedly Japanese.

The city of Honolulu has also been attacked, and considerable damage done. This battle has been going on for nearly three hours. One of the bombs dropped within 50 feet of KGU tower. It is no joke. It is a real war.

The public of Honolulu has been advised to keep in their homes and await results from the Army and Navy. There has been fierce fighting going on in the air and on the sea. The heavy shooting seems to be — one, two, three, four. Just a moment. We'll interrupt here.

We cannot estimate yet how much damage has been done, but it has been a very severe attack. And the Navy and Army appear now to have the air and the sea under control." [1]

We all froze as we listened. Even the *Issei* women, whose English skills were poor, stopped working, sensing that something was wrong. Margarita, Jits and I looked at each other, not moving as the words fell upon us.

---

[1] NBC News, December 7, 1941.

When the report was over, Jits was the first to speak. "It can't be that bad. It's the Japanese, not us. We're Americans. They can't do anything to us."

"You don't think so, Jits? We might be unpleasantly surprised, yah?" Margarita replied with her superior look. I looked between the two.

I was about ready to say, *We're Americans, what can they do? Ben's joining the US Army, for goodness sake. He's signed up to fight for America.* But my eyes focused beyond Jits and Margarita to my mother and her friends at their table. Those ladies, who had only moments ago been talking and laughing just like us girls, had been here in America for over 20 years. Those ladies had stopped working, one of them asking girls at a younger table to translate what they had just heard. And I realized that those ladies weren't Americans, couldn't be Americans, because of the laws that said Japanese couldn't become naturalized citizens. They were Aliens.

Later they would be called Enemy Aliens.